STAR TREK®: CROSSWORDS

Book 1

Boldly going where no solver has gone before,
50 enterprising new crosswords to challenge your *Star Trek* knowledge.

Edited by John M. Samson

POCKET BOOKS

New York   London   Toronto   Sydney   Singapore   Alpha Centauri

John M. Samson is considered by many to be the leading crossword puzzle editor working today. After many years of collaboration with the legendary Eugene T. Maleska, John took over sole editorship of the Simon & Schuster Crossword Puzzle Series following Maleska's death. John is also a prolific contributor of puzzles to a wide variety of specialty publications and newspapers where his work is always in great demand. An enthusiast of movies, music and drama, John is also very much the family man and likes to spend as much time as he can away from the puzzle business with his wife and two children.

Sam Bellotto Jr. is a recognized name in crosswords, a successful software developer and a lifelong science fiction enthusiast. He has been selling puzzles professionally since the late 1970s. Sam is also the force behind Crossdown, a small software development company that produces award-winning crossword, acrostic and cryptogram hobby and game products sold as shareware around the world. When not at the computer or making puzzles, Sam likes to go for short jogs, shovel snow and grow raspberries.

Raymond Hamel has been devoted to the pursuit of trivia since hosting a live trivia show in college in 1979. This endeavor has led him to writing and hosting weekly trivia shows on radio stations in La Crosse, Wisconsin and Madison, Wisconsin. Ray has also applied his trivia mind to crosswords, to date having published more than 1,100 of them. By day, Ray is a special collections librarian at the University of Wisconsin. When not working on a puzzle, you might find him playing disc golf or with a guitar in hand.

ACROSS

1 Bajoran cat
5 Medic for a colony of ex-Borg in "Unity" [VGR]
9 Author Bombeck
13 Use an energy containment cell
15 Kind of carvings in "Shadowplay" [DS9]
16 God-like computer in "The Apple" [TOS]
17 Arachnid with half-meter-long legs
19 Dax symbiont who succeeded Jadzia
20 Teer on Capella IV in "Friday's Child" [TOS]
21 Be a breadwinner
23 Spanish wave
24 2024 San Francisco problem
26 Science station Tango ___
28 PC alphanumeric abbr.
31 Scuffle
33 Taxi
34 Like 17 Across
36 Omicron ___ star system
39 Assault weapon
40 T'Lani government envoy in "Armageddon Game" [DS9]
43 Opposite of dep.
44 Whitewashed
46 ___ targ (Klingon dishes)
48 Shogun capital
49 Bajoran poet Akorem in "Accession" [DS9]
50 Elevator inventor
51 Homeworld of two assassins sent to DS9 in "Babel"
53 Leader before Lenin
55 Aldorian beverage served in Ten-Forward
56 Mass. motto word
58 ___ wing-slug
61 ___ caves of No'Mat
63 Lifeform indigenous to the Orillian homeworld
66 Lt. Paris spent time here
67 Radiate
68 Fesarius commander who offered Kirk tranya
69 Klaang escaped from one in "Broken Bow" [ENT]
70 Caps for Scotty
71 Billionth: Prefix

DOWN

1 English royal letters
2 Samoan friend of Jadzia Dax
3 Chess castle
4 Base where the Magellan crew put on a talent show
5 Ndefo who played Drex
6 Used a travel pod
7 Restless
8 Star Trek: Enterprise Supervising Producer Howard
9 Brenner in "Violations" [TNG]
10 Tarkassian imaginary friend of Guinan as a child
11 McGivers who befriends Khan in "Space Seed" [TOS]
12 Saturn ender
14 Actor Morales
18 "___ and Loss" [DS9]
22 Alpha-currant ___
25 Salver
27 Superdome shout
28 Member of Klingon Intelligence in "Visionary" [DS9]
29 Style of regime on Ekos in "Patterns of Force" [TOS]
30 Denebian creature Korax compared to Kirk
32 Parent of P'Chan in "Survival Instinct" [VGR]
35 Modernized
37 Deanna on Star Trek: The Next Generation
38 Pound sounds
41 Warp core reactor output
42 Captain of the U.S.S. Equinox also in the Delta Quadrant
45 Author LeShan
47 Tactical officer on night shift in "Rightful Heir" [TNG]
49 Bajoran grain-processing center
51 Kes is kidnapped to this planet in "Warlord" [VGR]
52 Tanandra Bay, for one
54 Show horse
55 Priestly robes
57 "Inter Arma ___ Silent Leges" [DS9]
59 Sect of the Kazon Collective
60 Miles O'Brien's coffee-cutoff hour
62 Of old
64 Gigatons: Abbr.
65 Fight finisher

Sam Bellotto Jr.

ACROSS

1 *The Jungle* author Sinclair
6 Trentin in "The Darkness and the Light" [DS9]
10 Parley in "Sacred Ground" [VGR]
14 Starship's course, say
15 Tuvok's wife
16 Sensors are ___-directional
17 Data's ship in "Redemption, Part II" [TNG]
19 Smidgens
20 Literary detective Lupin
21 Cereal box abbr.
22 Soldier ___'Taral in "Hippocratic Oath" [DS9]
23 Klingon worm dish
25 Extradition judge in "Dax" [DS9]
27 Martus Mazur took his gambling device in "Rivals" [DS9]
30 Horse chow
31 He played Flint in "Requiem for Methuselah" [TOS]
32 "Someone to Watch ___ Me" [DS9]
34 Tsunkatse match organizer [VGR]
36 *TNG* episode that introduced Third of Five
40 Federation Ambassador in "The Trouble With Tribbles" [TOS]
42 It was operated by Brynner Information Systems [DS9]
43 Friend of Will Riker in "Inside Man" [VGR]
44 Hit a Texas leaguer
45 "Woe is me!"
47 Klingon mercenary in "Invasive Procedures" [DS9]
48 Ferengi after Barzan wormhole rights in "The Price" [TNG]
50 Kahmar's son in "Apocalypse Rising" [DS9]
52 Astrometrics ___
53 Starship class that included the *Grissom* and *Vico*
56 Striped stone
58 Garrison of tennis
59 Sisko's fellow officer on the *U.S.S. Okinawa*
61 *Star Trek: Voyager* officer seen in "Hunters"
65 Related
66 Starship on which Ensign Ro served
68 Give a little
69 Give off, as chroniton particles
70 Drayan played by Tahj Mowry in "Innocence" [VGR]
71 Latin wings
72 *Pleeka* ___, casserole material used by Neelix
73 Ktarian operative ___ Jol in "The Game" [TNG]

DOWN

1 Stellar bear
2 Serve the Romulan ale
3 Sounds of disapproval
4 "By Any ___ Name" [TOS]
5 Town near Green Bay
6 Capable of warp speed: Abbr.
7 In pieces
8 Impart
9 Gul Danar's warship in "Past Prologue" [DS9]
10 Khan's sleeper ship in "Space Seed" [TOS]
11 Security officer killed by Garak in "Empok Nor" [DS9]
12 Talarian who raised Jono in "Suddenly Human" [TNG]
13 Eva Loseth's role in "Life Support" [DS9]
18 News summary
24 Animals that resemble Neelix
26 Garak's first name
27 Julie in 4 Down
28 Shape of *Voyager's* saucer section
29 ___-amino readout
31 Traditional Klingon warrior's knife
33 Runabout stationed at Deep Space 9
35 Apgar in "A Matter of Perspective" [TNG]
37 City S of Moscow
38 Ensign Tannenbaum
39 Liquid lump
41 Data's pet cat
46 *Voyager* conn officer killed in the debut episode
49 Sonic ___
51 "Pronto!"
53 Scientist killed by the Vians in "The Empath" [TOS]
54 He played Worf's human father
55 Wife of Gen. Ardelon Tantro in "Dax" [DS9]
56 Promenade shopkeeper Lysia on DS9
57 Disease that would spell trouble for tribbles
60 One of Icheb's playmates
62 Black: Latin
63 Wear out
64 Starfleet officer Karapleedeez
67 British inc.

Raymond Hamel

ACROSS

1 No friends of Robin Hood
5 Zephyr
9 "The Schizoid ___" [TNG]
12 Zeon resistance fighter in "Patterns of Force" [TOS]
14 Netsuke container
15 Ensign Ro Laren's father
16 He portrayed groundskeeper Boothby
18 Like Zobral's planet in "Desert Crossing" [ENT]
19 Cockney man of the hour
20 Shout from the bleachers
21 Reviews
23 ___ reticular stimulation
25 Scarfe who played Augris in "Resistance" [VGR]
26 Son of Col. Christopher in "Tomorrow Is Yesterday" [TOS]
29 Earthquake-related
31 Planet where Bendera met Chakotay in "Alliances" [VGR]
33 Dr. Apgar and others
34 Fitting
37 Grammy winner Mardin
38 Part of TNT
40 Miles O'Brien's homeland
41 ___ Officer Chang
42 Miracle site in John 2:1
43 Voyager Executive Producer Rick
45 Sexual maturation in Ocampa females
48 Animals in "Bread and Circuses" [TOS]
49 "___ of Evil" [TNG]
50 Bajoran Basso who got comfort women for Terok Nor
52 They observe Rules of Acquisition
54 Bajoran supreme religious leader
55 Subcommander in "The Enterprise Incident" [TOS]
58 Darwin's___in of the Species
59 She portrayed Marla McGivers in "Space Seed" [TOS]
62 Daughter of King Aleus
63 Indium's "49": Abbr.
64 Where Spock's mother is from
65 Marseilles Mrs.
66 Impending
67 Friends of Robin Hood

DOWN

1 Like crystalline dilithium
2 Building beam
3 ___-stasis units
4 Why?
5 "If ___ Were Horses" [DS9]
6 Tiny colonist
7 Star Trek V: The Final ___
8 Up ___ good
9 He portrayed Gul Dukat
10 Wormhole ___
11 Quint and Romero
13 Sirtis in The Next Generation
15 Quark's cousin
17 White-handed gibbon
22 Skye caps
23 Flub a chip shot
24 Starship that fires on Sisko in "A Time to Stand" [DS9]
26 RN's "at once!"
27 Starship named for a Greek goddess
28 The Borg queen in Star Trek: First Contact
30 Grunge
32 Obstruction
35 Husband of Juliana Tainer
36 Human number base
39 Arjin studying under Dax in "Playing God" [DS9]
40 Alternate reality son of Worf and Deanna
42 Flight controller, for short
44 She died of old age at 27 in "The Deadly Years" [TOS]
46 Lord of the manor
47 He tells Torres to eat heart of targ in "Day of Honor" [VGR]
49 McCoy made one in "The Deadly Years" [TOS]
51 "___ you die well" (Klingon parting words)
52 Root beer head
53 FBI agent
55 "Comin' ___ the Rye"
56 Prefix for destruct or pilot
57 Annealing oven
60 It was seeded galaxy-wide in "The Chase" [TNG]
61 Hip-hop

Sam Bellotto Jr.

ACROSS

1 Federation Ambassador to Qo'noS
5 Admiral in "The Dogs of War" [DS9]
9 Hood played by Picard in "QPid" [TNG]
14 Forest ox
15 Like the Borg
16 Heavenly prefix
17 Elasian love-potion drop ("Elaan of Troyius" [TOS])
18 Meyer in *Star Trek Nemesis*
19 Barber in "Schisms" [TNG]
20 Tuvok portrayer
22 *Star Trek: Deep Space Nine* star
24 Suffix for differ
25 West's "Diamond" role
26 Forename of 46 Across
30 She plays T'Pol
34 City S of Moscow
35 Shinzon's adopted home
37 Christmas
38 French goose
39 Ocampan rescued by Neelix in "Caretaker" [VGR]
40 U.S. 3-R's org.
41 Theology degrees
43 William Riker's J'naii love ("The Outcast" [TNG])
45 Sing jazz
46 *The Final Frontier* director
48 Twin butterfly ___ in "Broken Bow" [ENT]
50 Shoe width
51 ___ chi (martial art)
52 "This Side of Paradise" hazards [TOS]
56 *Voyager* captain
60 Like the Great Hall of Qam-Chee
61 Saurians have three on each foot
63 Seven of Nine's cortical ___
64 "Do ___ to eat a peach?": Eliot
65 Aunt in "Caretaker, Part 1" [VGR]
66 Dr. Crusher's lab wear
67 Dapper
68 Tyree's wife ("A Private Little War" [TOS])
69 Sailor's saint

DOWN

1 After tera or giga
2 "The ___ Love": Jolson hit
3 Wander
4 She's Jadzia Dax
5 Dwarf in "Time and Again" [VGR]
6 Sheep genus
7 "Let He Who Is Without ___ ..." [DS9]
8 Pole, e.g.
9 Pavel Chekov's homeland
10 Gowron portrayer
11 Insulation strip
12 "Tacking ___ the Wind" [DS9]
13 Film ___
21 Prefix for matrix
23 Misfortunes
26 Grant in "Arena" [TOS]
27 Whiskey drank by Picard
28 She married Rom
29 Gul Dukat's son [DS9]
30 Cleared the table
31 Eighth of a cup
32 Like carvino juice
33 Poet inspired by Onaya in "The Muse" [DS9]
36 Debussy's *La ___*
42 *Nemesis* star
43 Lady Morella, for one
44 Yar from Turkana IV
45 T'Pol's field
47 Lisa in "Rocks and Shoals" [DS9]
49 Martin in "Haven" [TNG]
52 Quark's uncle
53 Aldean in "When the Bough Breaks" [TNG]
54 Klingon military academy [TNG]
55 Orega in "The Outrageous Okona" [TNG]
56 Simmons who was Admiral Norah Satie
57 Vitarian ___ underwear
58 Dr. Sevrin's follower who sought Eden [TOS]
59 Klingon mercenary hired by Verad [DS9]
62 He sleeps in a bucket

John M. Samson

ACROSS

1 *Nemesis* hero
5 Farpoint Station, for example
9 Launch ___
12 Krige in *First Contact*
14 Mild cheese
15 Gauze weave
16 Planet where Dr. Stubbs wanted to take Deanna
18 "Once More ___ the Breach" [DS9]
19 Barcelona bear
20 Punzo-___-roku match in "The Icarus Factor" [TNG]
21 Kind of beam
23 Yeoman Ross in "The Squire of Gothos" [TOS]
25 Estuaries
26 Teer in "Friday's Child" [TOS]
29 "The City on the Edge of ___" [TOS]
31 False reality creator in "Future Imperfect" [TNG]
33 Refrain syllables
34 *U.S.S. Voyager* in "Future's End, Part II" [VGR]
37 Small raise?
38 Star cluster in "Too Short a Season" [TNG]
40 Letters of urgency
41 Biblical ending for lead
42 Antitoxins
43 Sirtis who plays Deanna Troi
45 Karidian Players member
48 M. ___ Hudec (Majel Barrett)
49 Allasomorph from Daled IV in "The Dauphin" [TNG]
50 Bajoran colony governor in "Heart of Stone" [DS9]
52 Ship destroyed by Klingons in *Star Trek III: The Search for Spock*
54 Jack Ryan's org.
55 Meaty sandwich
58 Remainder
59 Planet where Picard was kidnapped
62 Cuckoos
63 Picard Mozart ___, program 1
64 *Enterprise-D* executive officer
65 Dallas NBAer
66 Glacial mounds
67 Writer Roddenberry

DOWN

1 Game of chance in Quark's bar
2 Aldorian brews
3 Tenor Schipa
4 Oh, in Oldenburg
5 Topic of "The Hands of the Prophets" [DS9]
6 Summer hrs. in Nova Scotia
7 People who hate mysteries in "The Chase" [TNG]
8 Dubai leader
9 Nenebek crash site in "Final Mission" [TNG]
10 Dryworms' planet ___ IV
11 A servo opens this
13 Lawn tools
15 Capt. Janeway's holo-character
17 A Bajoran's is jeweled
22 Nodes that resemble ramscoops
23 Ferengi DaiMon in "The Last Outpost" [TNG]
24 Where mediator Riva succeeded
26 Nichols' protagonist
27 German philosopher
28 Homeworld of Chekov's imaginary brother Piotr
30 Cardassian Garak on Deep Space 9
32 Yesterday, in Paris
35 Mugato tooth
36 Moonfish
39 Hyper-REM sleepers
40 ___ of blackness
42 DS9 et al.: Abbr.
44 Planetary system in "Amok Time" [TOS]
46 Swellings
47 Selcundi Drema or Archanis
49 *TOS* episode where Kirk fights the Gorn
51 Don't call Janeway this
52 0.035 ounce
53 Nona- less one
55 Exercycle
56 Kes portrayer in *Voyager*
57 Fatigue
60 Debussy's "Air de ___"
61 Mr., in Roma

Sam Bellotto Jr.

ACROSS

1 Nacelle support
6 Dr. McCoy's predecessor
11 Tweedle-___
14 Mind-controlling Bajoran in "Repression" [VGR]
15 Good-bye, in Picard's homeland
16 Worf's was affected in "Parallels" [TNG]
17 Added to the Borg collective
19 Tayback in "A Piece of the Action" [TOS]
20 "The ___ Degree" [TNG]
21 He helped Kira escape in "Second Skin" [DS9]
22 Give a speech
24 Ajilon Prime, e.g. ("Nor the Battle to the Strong" [DS9])
28 Foil firm
31 Like Ensign Janice Rand
32 Morn's business associate [DS9]
33 "Stop that!"
34 Stumblebum
37 Charlie X, for one
38 Jaunty
39 Nodes of Tosk's ship [DS9]
40 Starship's CNS
41 Track units
42 Capt. Garrett in "Yesterday's Enterprise" [TNG]
43 Cor ___ V, attacked by the Phyrox plague [TNG]
46 Black-and-white animal
47 TOS episode with Spock playing the Vulcan lute
51 Hirogen ___ station
52 Soble of "Spectre of the Gun" [TOS]
53 Part of MPH
56 Building wing
57 Gorgan in "And the Children Shall Lead" [TOS]
62 Entity in "Justice" [TNG]
63 Medical researcher in "Dear Doctor" [ENT]
64 Al-Batani's expedition
65 German article
66 Female android created by Flint [TOS]
67 Deep Space 9 security officer

DOWN

1 Getz of jazz
2 Transporter ___ article
3 Military advisor in "Warlord" [VGR]
4 ___'lash, Brunt's servant in "Profit and Lace" [DS9]
5 Romulan commander in "The Enemy" [TNG]
6 Ballerina who loved Dr. Bashir [DS9]
7 She's sweet as apple cider
8 Prison inmate in "The Chute" [VGR]
9 Shoe box letters
10 Dancer Nureyev
11 Inventor of the cardiac procedure that saved Picard's life
12 What the Federation worlds did
13 Cardassian commander in "The Wounded" [TNG]
18 Dr. Graves in "The Schizoid Man" [TNG]
23 Arctic explorer
24 Quark's concern
25 Zodiac sign
26 Nechani holy men in "Sacred Ground" [VGR]
27 Compassion
28 ___-jytsu (unarmed combat)
29 Fat from hogs
30 Assassination victim in Star Trek VI: The Undiscovered Country
33 Given a hand of fizzbin
35 Enthusiastic
36 Trentin in "The Darkness and the Light" [DS9]
38 Strategic action
39 ___ 7 in "A Taste of Armageddon" [TOS]
42 Ten-Forward has one
44 Xepolite captain Drofo ___ in "The Maquis, Part II" [DS9]
45 Destiny captain in "Afterimage" [DS9]
47 Cornered
48 She played Takar in "Scientific Method" [VGR]
49 Flores who played Marissa in "Disaster" [TNG]
50 Keefer in "Assignment: Earth" [TOS]
53 Ballet move
54 Homeworld of the Dohlman [TOS]
55 Voyager episode about asteroids
58 Spanish pronoun
59 Secular
60 Dr. Simon ___ Gelder
61 Palindromic preposition

Raymond Hamel

ACROSS

1 *U.S.S. Thunderchild's* class
6 Arton and Carlson
11 Thrice: Comb. form
14 "Battle ___" [DS9]
15 White as ___
16 Outlaw in "A Fistful of Datas" [TNG]
17 Towing mechanism aboard spacecraft
19 Scapegrace
20 Twin world orbiting Omega Sagitta
21 Picard carved "A.F." in one
22 Witch
23 Medical scans in "Projections" [VGR]
25 Reason for using anesthizine gas
28 Country singer White
31 Cow calls
33 Milne marsupial
34 Cardassian detention center
36 Freighter captain's species in "The Abandoned" [DS9]
39 Alley-___
40 Jonathan Archer's rank
42 Columbus campus
43 Sarek's homeworld
45 Holo-novel character in "Heroes and Demons" [VGR]
47 Ending for tutor
48 Kiddies
49 *Jane ___*: Brontë
50 *S.S. Botany Bay's* power source
53 Bard of Avon: Abbr.
55 "So, there you are!"
56 Semi
58 Asimov who inspired Dr. Soong
61 Violin string
62 Technology distrusted by McCoy
65 Tail: Comb. form
66 Bajoran hero Li
67 Traditional Japanese food
68 *Cleponji* Captain Galek in "Booby Trap" [TNG]
69 Puffs of wind
70 Valakian hospital director in "Dear Doctor" [ENT]

DOWN

1 PC key
2 Meru or Nerys
3 ___ the finish
4 Get back
5 Jeremy in "The Bonding" [TNG]
6 Jolt
7 Hamburg's river
8 Words after force and energy
9 Spican ___ gem
10 Together: Prefix
11 Starling's quest in "Future's End" [VGR]
12 The Dohlman's home planet
13 Klingon forehead feature
18 Like Kes
24 Alterian chowder, e.g.
26 "Cold ___" [ENT]
27 Memnon's mother
28 10th-century Pope
29 Felipe of baseball
30 Food source on a starship
32 Word form of "upright"
35 Richter's ___ of culture
36 Vessel used by Species 8472
37 Munich river
38 Dr. Moset's Fostossa virus quest
41 What Mrs. Narsu teaches
44 Lt. Cmdr. Hudson
46 Corridor in which DaiMon Prak got standed
48 "___ and Tribble-ations" [DS9]
50 Ferengi master of commerce
51 Kirk's communications officer
52 Pianist Claudio
54 Together
57 Biting fly
59 "___ boy!"
60 U.S. jobs program
62 Capt. Picard series, for short
63 Hissing sound
64 Korean soldier

Sam Bellotto Jr.

ACROSS

1 Lissepian Mother's Day Heist target [DS9]
5 "___ Soil" [TNG]
9 ___ IV, planet in "The Dauphin" [TNG]
14 Rapier
15 Arethian flu symptom
16 In the know
17 Hammett terrier
18 Space pocket in "The Outcast" [TNG]
19 Deneb II serial murderer in "Wolf in the Fold" [TOS]
20 "Whom Gods ___" [TOS]
22 Atom ___
24 Mallet used in parrises squares "Real Life" [VGR]
25 Nobel-winning UN agency: Abbr.
26 "The Return of the Archons" betrayer [TOS]
30 Like Benaren or Martis [VGR]
34 Ferengi arms merchant in "Unification, Part II" [TNG]
35 ___ II, planet home of Armus in "Skin of Evil" [TNG]
37 Dublin locale
38 Ambassador Alkar [TNG]
39 Optolythic data ___
40 In accordance with
41 Ba'ku friend of Picard in *Star Trek Insurrection*
43 David ___ Stiers in "Half a Life" [TNG]
45 Canadian photographer Roloff
46 Jean ___ Aroeste, "All Our Yesterdays" [TOS] writer
48 Father of Tarrana in "Homeward" [TNG]
50 "___ He Who Is Without Sin ..." [DS9]
51 *Fal-tor-___*, Vulcan ritual
52 Tarsus IV colonist in "The Conscience of the King" [TOS]
56 Esaak portrayer in 13 Down
60 ___ Blin, Bajoran official in "Babel" [DS9]
61 Dala conned him in "Live Fast and Prosper" [VGR]
63 Pinza of opera
64 "Return to ___" [DS9]
65 Seven of Nine's mother
66 Singha refugee ___
67 Ch'Tang officer in "Once More Unto the Breach" [DS9]
68 Mulgrew of *Voyager*
69 What Golanga injured in "Paradise" [DS9]

DOWN

1 Andarian glass ___
2 Church recess
3 Gravitic sensor grids in "Face of the Enemy" [TNG]
4 Dominic of *Enterprise*
5 Planet in "Basics, Part I and II" [VGR]
6 ___ Jel in "Crossfire" [DS9]
7 Penthor-___ in "The Vengeance Factor" [TNG]
8 Klabnian life-forms detested by Q
9 "Rogue Planet" planet [ENT]
10 Like the powers of Q
11 Wield the *ahn-woon*
12 ___ Stanley Gardner
13 "___ Doctor" [ENT]
21 Fish eggs
23 Isinglass
26 Cardassian planet in 64 Across
27 Tuvok's mother
28 *Enterprise* episode
29 Like the Algorian mammoth
30 Wogneer creatures' home nebula in "Allegiance" [TNG]
31 Dr. McCoy's predecessor
32 *TOS* episode where Kirk fought the Gorn
33 Kira of *Deep Space Nine*
36 "Playing ___" [DS9]
42 Captain of the *U.S.S. Cairo*
43 Genetic "superman" in "Space Seed" [TOS]
44 Planet in "The Learning Curve" [VGR]
45 Martin ___, Genome Colonist on Moab IV [TNG]
47 ___ III, Federation planet in "Cost of Living" [TNG]
49 Betazoid Elbrun in "Tin Man" [TNG]
52 Bacon go-with at Quark's
53 Crosby who played Natima Lang
54 ___'Vora (the shared heart) in "The Disease" [VGR]
55 He kidnapped Troi in "Face of the Enemy" [TNG]
56 Nahsk's brother in "Who Mourns for Morn?" [DS9]
57 Rebi's brother in "Collective" [VGR]
58 Green Terran fruit
59 Jog
62 Scan in "Projections" [VGR]

John M. Samson

ACROSS

1 *Voyager* peril in "Night" [VGR]
5 DaiMon in "Force of Nature" [TNG]
9 Rind
13 Karapleedeez killed in "Conspiracy" [TNG]
14 A mugato has one on its head
15 Alfarian hair ___
16 Himalayan mystery
17 Langston Hughes poem
18 Dohlman of Troyius
19 *D'deridex* class ship in "The Neutral Zone" [TNG]
22 Kolaish spice ___
23 Quark's nephew
24 Latin goddess
25 Less plentiful
30 Relatives
32 SE Texas college
33 Moue
35 Tox ___ (quantum phase inverter)
39 Artificially generated tunnel to the Gamma Quadrant
43 Commanding officer on Deep Space 9
44 Dying race in *Insurrection*
45 Lya IV, for one: Abbr.
46 Holodeck outlaw in "A Fistful of Datas" [TNG]
48 Stun settings are ___
51 Airline monogram
54 Reed and Yar, e.g.: Abbr.
56 Caesar's 250
57 George and Gracie in *Star Trek IV: The Voyage Home*
63 Kirk's communications officer
64 Ouse feeder
65 Bajoran framed in "Ensign Ro" [TNG]
67 Phaser forerunner
68 Remus Rabbit
69 *E pluribus___*
70 Compass points
71 ___ serif
72 Odo portrayer Auberjonois

DOWN

1 Series after *TNG*
2 Real standout
3 "Tacking ___ the Wind" [DS9]
4 Title given to Ferengi leaders
5 Attorney Louvois in "The Measure of a Man" [TNG]
6 Roster
7 Eisenberg who plays 23 Across
8 Completely understood
9 Bajoran food server Daier on Terok Nor
10 Flag seen in "The Royal" [TNG]
11 Fixed look
12 Planetary system in the El-Adrel sector
15 Rare mineral mined on Janus VI
20 Mutual-fund type: Abbr.
21 NASA "thumbs-up"
25 *Red October* et al.
26 Wine shed
27 Thesaurus abbrs.
28 Geologic periods
29 He wanted to collapse the wormhole in "Visionary" [DS9]
31 "The ___ Degree" [TNG]
34 ___ avail (futile)
36 Humanoid Trill part
37 Utah ski spot
38 Mallard relative
40 Aso ___ (Nigerian attire)
41 Feature on *Miranda*-class vessels
42 Cattlemen
47 "Give ___ rest!"
49 Liquidator Brunt's org.
50 "___ Yesterdays" [TOS]
51 *Enterprise* technician in "Space Seed" [TOS]
52 City in E China
53 Entertain
55 Strikebreakers
58 Federation VIP: Abbr.
59 Visitor in *Deep Space Nine*
60 Brown who played Kohlar on "Prophecy" [VGR]
61 Enniskillen river
62 Phaser setting
66 French soul

Sam Bellotto Jr.

ACROSS

1 Maters
5 Eucalyptus eater
10 Nickname Sulu hated
14 One of the Borg children on *Voyager*
15 One of the Great Lakes
16 Part of the *Enterprise* destruct sequence
17 Yepremian of football
18 Cake topping
19 Bryn ___
20 Episode Chekhov is tortured by Klingons
23 Athletically stellar
24 Earhart and Lindbergh, e.g.
28 Lizard genus
30 Martin in "Haven" [TNG]
31 "Obsession" [TOS] writer Wallace
32 Yankee Stadium area
37 "Begone!"
38 Episode Chekov is killed
42 Like the *U.S.S. Enterprise CV-N*
43 Tarsus IV, e.g.
44 "Grok"
45 Network with VJs
48 Sulan's work place ("Faces" [VGR])
49 Heavenly
52 ___ Haro, false Bajoran in "Allegiance" [TNG]
57 Episode Chekov is put into the agony booth
59 Shortest *Star Trek* episode title
62 Peep show
63 Ahab's father
64 DaiMon in "Ferengi Love Songs" [DS9]
65 "Suspicions" actress Tricia [TNG]
66 Rescue
67 Warrior Danar in "The Hunted" [TNG]
68 Orange peels
69 List-ending abbr.

DOWN

1 One of "Mudd's Women" [TOS]
2 Ambassador in "Drive" [VGR]
3 She possessed Seven in "Infinite Regress" [VGR]
4 Pry
5 2293 peace conference site
6 Toe-stubbing cry
7 Federation starship *NCC-45167*
8 Author seen in "Time's Arrow" [TNG]
9 SW African republic
10 Oscar-winner Marisa
11 "Ship ___ Bottle" [TNG]
12 "___ Ground" [TNG]
13 Denise Crosby role
21 Uttaberries, e.g.
22 Rocketeer Wernher ___ Braun
25 Bajoran child in "Tears of the Prophets" [DS9]
26 Rainbow fish
27 Like Worf's visage, frequently
29 Romulan ___
32 Inedible orange
33 Agitated
34 Spock's teddy bear had these
35 "Family Business" gp. [DS9]
36 Screen thriller of 1950
37 Jiffy
39 Capable of warp speed: abbr.
40 Confines
41 Kazon sect in "Manuevers" [VGR]
45 Medical scanner
46 "Balance of ___" [TOS]
47 Bajoran musician in "Sanctuary" [DS9]
50 ___ II, planet in "A Matter of Perspective" [TNG]
51 Astronaut Shriver
53 Kalin in "The Host" [TNG]
54 Bajoran artist Zimm in "Fascination" [DS9]
55 Blight victim in "The Quickening" [DS9]
56 Ramsey's mate in "Angel One" [TNG]
58 Ryan in "Power Play" [TNG]
59 Former space station
60 Sector studied in "Realm of Fear" [TNG]
61 Barclay in "Pathfinder" [VGR]

Raymond Hamel

ACROSS

1 Turner of American history
4 Like another *Enterprise* in *The Voyage Home*
9 Bird sound
14 "New" time period in "Death Wish" [VGR]
15 Come ___ (mature)
16 *Enterprise* helmsman in "That Which Survives" [TOS]
17 Nonaligned peoples in "The Maquis" [DS9]
19 Tarkalean condor nest
20 Like the J'naii race in "The Outcast" [TNG]
21 *DS9* episode in which Jonathan Frakes guested
23 Suliban who befriends Archer in "Broken Bow" [ENT]
24 End for depend
25 Letter abbr.
27 Breen General in "Strange Bedfellows" [DS9]
29 Numerical prefix
33 Starfleet pilot killed by Chu'lak in "Field of Fire" [DS9]
36 Matt in "The Darkness and the Light" [DS9]
37 Psychiatrist who assisted Kirk in "Dagger of the Mind" [TOS]
38 Saint-___-l'École
39 Wesley Crusher's date in "Sarek" [TNG]
42 British corp.
43 Tandaran Major in "Detained" [ENT]
45 "Winter of Artifice" author
46 Goblins
48 Klingon mercenary in "Invasive Procedure" [DS9]
49 New England cape
50 "Message ___ Bottle" [VGR]
51 Roman 16
53 Org.
57 Monitoring station in *Star Trek: The Motion Picture*
61 Orion ___ woman
62 Chateau ___ champagne
63 Communications Officer aboard *Enterprise NX-01*
65 Corridor
66 After pan or scout
67 Lidell who accuses Paris of murder in "Ex Post Facto" [VGR]
68 Subordinate Hirogen pack members
69 Betazoid survivor in "Night Terrors" [TNG]

70 Three, in Roma

DOWN

1 Energy ribbon in *Star Trek Generations*
2 *Star Trek: The Original Series* episode where Kirk fights the Gorn
3 Sumatran animal
4 Commander Zlangco's species in "Battle Lines" [DS9]
5 In ___ (troubled)
6 Tulaberry wine cask
7 Like Pulaski in "Unnatural Selection" [TNG]
8 ___ majesty
9 What Tuvok must do in "Learning Curve" [VGR]
10 Wesley Crusher portrayer in *Nemesis*
11 Take home
12 Improve a mansucript
13 ___ kwon do
18 Willow
22 Alien species in "Acquisition" [ENT]
26 Klingon High ___
27 ___ Nagus
28 Suffix for ball
30 Meany on *Deep Space Nine*
31 Head of France
32 Auto pioneer

33 Like *gagh*, to some
34 1988 Masters winner
35 Smell ___ (suspect)
40 Akritinian prisoner with Kim and Paris in "The Chute" [VGR]
41 Amber-colored ale in "Time Squared" [TNG]
44 *Enterprise* episode with an amorphous alien
47 *Enterprise* episode with Rene Auberjonois
52 Thorny predators on Surata IV [TNG]
54 Like Wesley Crusher
55 Western
56 Ibudan in "A Man Alone" [DS9]
57 Peace Nobelist Wiesel
58 Cardassian vole, for one
59 "Here's trouble!"
60 Leonhardt in "Eye of the Beholder" [TNG]
61 "Alas!"
62 Leonard Nimoy once drove one
64 Sink down

Sam Bellotto Jr.

ACROSS

1 German officer in "The Killing Game, Part I" [VGR]
5 Cardassian outpost in "Past Prologue" [DS9]
9 She played Dr. Renhol in "Equilibrium" [DS9]
14 Persis Khambatta role in *The Motion Picture*
15 Yalies
16 Aunt of Jean-Luc Picard
17 ___ beacon, high-beam flashlight
18 Has the Thelusian flu
19 Island off Venezuela
20 Planet seeders in "The Paradise Syndrome" [TOS]
23 Starbase "II" location in "The Offspring" [TNG]
24 Cal Hudson in "The Maquis, Part I" [DS9]
25 What 14 Across lacked
27 Help to the brig
30 Prah ___, in "Cold Front" [ENT]
33 Bend down
34 Greville Henwood role in "Terra Nova" [ENT]
36 Stanley Cup org.
37 Retirees' org.
38 Gamma ___ II in "The Vengeance Factor" [TNG]
39 Bologna bye-bye
40 "Cause ___ Effect" [TNG]
41 Scalosian queen ("Wink of an Eye" [TOS])
42 Wood in "The Deadly Years" [TOS]
43 Obsidian Order member in "Defiant" [DS9]
45 ___ and Little Boy (1989)
46 ___ Kotay, Chakotay's alias in "Workforce, Part II" [VGR]
47 Southern Plains tribe
49 Race in "Rise" [VGR]
51 Guest of Trelane in "The Squire of Gothos" [TOS]
56 Kirk's love in "The City on the Edge of Forever" [TOS]
58 Small measure of matter
59 Spillane's ___ *Jury*
60 French annuity
61 *Saratoga* sister ship in "Emissary, Part I" [DS9]
62 McDonough in *First Contact*
63 Two bells, nautically
64 Snow vehicle
65 Water plant

DOWN

1 Merchant of Velos in "Critical Care" [VGR]
2 Winged
3 Make angry
4 Hydrogen collection device
5 San Simeon builder
6 Like Zefram Cochrane in "Metamorphosis" [TOS]
7 Offkey singer in "The Naked Time" [TOS]
8 The old country, to Chekov
9 Sheep's cry
10 Skillful
11 Incredibly dense matter
12 ___ II, rehab colony in "Whom Gods Destroy" [TOS]
13 Prepare kalo
21 Gunfighter in "Spectre of the Gun" [TOS]
22 "The Most Toys" [TNG] writer Goodhartz
26 "By ___ Other Name" [TOS]
27 Hospital director in "Dear Doctor" [ENT]
28 Comedian Riga in "The Outrageous Okona" [TNG]
29 Drug that revives Worf in "Ethics" [TNG]
30 Baby's cry
31 "Think Tank" [VGR] director Terrance
32 Fujisaki's protégé in "Inter Arma Enim Silent Leges" [DS9]
34 ___ IV, ship discovered in "One Small Step" [VGR]
35 Arridor's partner in "False Profits" [VGR]
38 She played Seltin in "Meridian" [DS9]
39 What Leonardo called Janeway ("Scorpion, Part I)
41 It was used to clone Kahless
42 Mowing site
44 Monk killed in "Accession" [DS9]
45 Frothed
47 Klingon smuggler in "Gambit, Part II" [TNG]
48 Holographic ___
49 Mad Roman emperor
50 "The Way to ___" [TOS]
52 "Silicon nodules" in "The Devil in the Dark" [TOS]
53 Jaret ___, in "Prime Factors" [VGR]
54 Carpet style
55 Human-Romulan hybrid in "Redemption, Part II" [TNG]
57 Uhura's was above her knees

Raymond Hamel

ACROSS

1 Picard's prison-mate in "Allegiance" [TNG]
6 Tyrant who escaped on the *S.S. Botany Bay*
10 Trek
14 Colony near the Bajoran system in "The Forsaken" [DS9]
15 Jane Austen novel
16 "Heroides" poet
17 Neelix' Kazon-Pommar contact in "Alliances" [VGR]
18 A rhea has six
19 Brent Spiner role
20 "___ to Psyche": Keats
21 Cologne article
23 Ro Laren, for one
25 Rivulet
26 "Shake ___!"
27 Scotty's negative
30 Vessel that exploded in "Legacy" [TNG]
32 Salon machine
36 "Trip" Tucker is one
38 Jameson's wife in "Too Short a Season" [TNG]
39 Kind of horizon in "Parallax" [VGR]
40 Gigaton's billion: Abbr.
42 Klingon leader poisoned by Duras ("Reunion" [TNG])
43 Catalog
44 "Doctor Bashir, ___" [DS9]
46 "___ Ego" [VGR]
48 Varnish
49 Cobb and Detmer
50 Newspaper section
52 Tent furnishing
53 "For the ___" [DS9]
56 Greek vowel
57 Kavarian tiger-___
60 Arm of the Amazon
61 Ex-Borg medic in "Unity" [VGR]
63 Samantha Wildman's daughter born on *Voyager*
65 Auricular
66 Suffix for Louis
67 Malevolent space probe in "The Changeling" [TOS]
68 Holo-character Nicky the ___
69 Deneb's constellation
70 Novan rescued by Archer in "Terra Nova" [ENT]

DOWN

1 Within: Comb. form
2 "Space ___" [TOS]
3 German river
4 P-T go-betweens
5 Region of space
6 ___-white (Jem'Hadar addiction)
7 Health plan
8 Andorian protozoans in "Tuvix" [VGR]: Var.
9 Of the proboscis
10 Vic Fontaine and The Doctor
11 ___ Prime (destroyed in "First Contact" [TNG])
12 Bajoran liaison to Deep Space 9
13 Dr. Sevrin's quest
22 Home to Miles O'Brien
24 Officer Turner on "CHiPs"
27 O'Brien's one-time Bajoran apprentice
28 Ear bone
29 Void
31 "Park" a starship near a planet
33 Unprocessed data
34 Klingons, to Kirk
35 Ocampa and Talaxians
37 *TNG* episode where Geordi's mother dies
41 Captain Proton, ___ First Class
42 Mythical home of the Skrreean race
45 Use for neurocine gas
47 Aussie hopper
48 Klingon ship in "Sleeping Dogs" [ENT]
51 Deanna and Lwaxana
53 "Once ___ a Time" [VGR]
54 20th-century defense pact
55 Bahr in "Endgame, Part I" [VGR]
57 Surviving crewman in "The Galileo Seven" [TOS]
58 Klingon cruiser destroyed by *V'Ger*
59 Shipshape
62 "___ voce poco fa": Rossini
64 Perfect at NASA

Sam Bellotto Jr.

ACROSS

1 *Pon farr*, e.g.
5 Planet in the Tellun system [TOS]
9 Couldn't help but
14 Swimming mammal
15 Lunch in a shell
16 "Time's ___" [TNG]
17 *Raison d'___*
18 Ba'ku woman in *Insurrection*
19 "Where ___ Has Gone Before" [TOS]
20 City where fans honor Capt. Kirk's birth
23 Chekov's old love in "The Way to Eden" [TOS]
24 Warp-speed abbr.
25 Grain used in developing quadrotriticale
28 Fox's home
29 ___ II, homeworld of Nellen Tore [TNG]
33 Mind-___, Klingon device
35 Luigi Amodeo in "The Cloud" [VGR]
37 Lt. Neeley in "Rocks and Shoals" [DS9]
38 Captain Janeway's hometown
41 Keiko O'Brien portrayer
43 Funds held by a third party
44 She played Ro Laren
47 Appear
48 Flavor enhancer: Abbr.
51 "___ That Be Your Last Battlefield" [TOS]
52 Ohm's reciprocal
54 Leonard James ___
56 Captain Picard's hometown
61 Music enjoyed by Worf
63 Kwan's supervisor in "Eye of the Beholder" [TNG]
64 What Spock and Kirk lacked for the bus in *The Voyage Home*
65 Archaeologist killed in "The Bonding" [TNG]
66 Vis-___
67 Mideast gulf
68 Vulcan admiral in "Favor the Bold" [DS9]
69 He played Beech in *Star Trek II: The Wrath of Khan*
70 Exposure units

DOWN

1 Computer access requirement, often
2 What Scotty did in 2294
3 Barkan IV inhabitant in 13 Down
4 Mother of 54 Across
5 Pilot announcements: Abbr.
6 T'___, people at war in "Armageddon Game" [DS9]
7 Horta secretion
8 Ba'ku man in *Insurrection*
9 Cor ___ V, planet in "Allegiance" [TNG]
10 In line
11 Medical officer in "Violations" [TNG]
12 ___ sheet
13 "Thine ___ Self" [TNG]
21 Shortwave device
22 "___ my first ray gun": Lily in *First Contact*
26 Aye
27 Historical period
30 "Alter ___" [VGR]
31 Capital of Togo
32 *VGR* episode about a false wormhole
34 Coladrium ___ in "Captive Pursuit" [DS9]
35 ___ fly, Klingon insect
36 "___ Upon a Time" [VGR]
38 DS9 officer killed in "Paradise Lost"
39 Test for a college sr.
40 Scotty's drinking partner ("By Any Other Name" [TOS])
41 Grey Cup org.
42 Gardening tool
45 Start a new mission
46 ___ Ka Ree
48 Galeo-___ style wrestling [DS9]
49 "___ Ground" [VGR]
50 Items in Neelix's kitchen
53 Resistance member in "Shakaar" [DS9]
55 Takarian in "False Profits" [VGR]
57 Region
58 Talk like Khan
59 Seven's human mother
60 "Live ___ and Prosper" [VGR]
61 New World treaty org.
62 ___ 2000, planet in "The Naked Time" [TOS]

Raymond Hamel

ACROSS

1 Sarpeidon librarian Mr. ___ ("All Our Yesterdays" [TOS])
5 Nezu traitor in "Rise" [VGR]
10 Samoan who danced at Jadzia's party
14 Tuvok played a Vulcan one
15 Work at 5 Down
16 Prohibits
17 Caen's river
18 Dr. Bashir sometimes induces these
20 Majel Barrett, ___ Hudec
21 *Kidnapped* author: Init.
22 Red Squad cadet Collins in "Valiant" [DS9]
23 Long-necked animal
26 Alaimo who plays Gul Dukat
27 Protector of Yaderan village in "Shadowplay" [DS9]
29 "Ex Post ___" [VGR]
33 Hall of Warriors honor
36 "___ That Be Your Last Battlefield" [TOS]
38 Data ___
39 Intelligent space entity in "Lonely Among Us" [TNG]
43 Miscalculate
44 "Ode ___ Nightingale": Keats
45 Spews lava
46 Like Neelix's bantan
49 Frequent reason for cryostasis
51 Seven-foot sisters once involved with Dax and Sisko
53 *U.S.S. Grissom* captain in *The Search for Spock*
57 Pilot 62 Across
60 Redman in *The Stand*
61 Matt who played Latha Mabrin [DS9]
62 Shuttlecraft built aboard *Voyager*
64 *Pon* ___ (Vulcan mating instinct)
65 Force ___ (draw)
66 Londoner's thread
67 "The ___ on the Edge of Forever" [TOS]
68 Rime
69 Facing a glacier
70 Duck genus

DOWN

1 "Move ___ Home" [DS9]
2 Hostile force in "Dragon's Teeth" [VGR]
3 Dr. Bejal in "Rejoined" [DS9]
4 Two after ex
5 Academy established in 2161
6 He portrayed McCoy
7 Drinks like Fido
8 Austrian "alas!"
9 *Enterprise* helmsman in "That Which Survives" [TOS]
10 Qomarian who liked the Doctor's singing in "Virtuoso" [VGR]
11 Kipling's "Rikki-Tikki-___"
12 Most draftable
13 Organization: Abbr.
19 Son of Mogh
24 Minutes
25 Number of mates in an Andorian marriage
26 Elec. Engineering deg.
28 Forearm bones
30 Chlorobicrobes increases this
31 Praise highly
32 Tote-board numbers
33 11°15' compass points: Abbr.
34 U. of Maryland mascot
35 Longfellow bell town
37 Repository of Lost ___ (Delta Quadrant junkyard)
40 Wife of Tieran in "Warlord" [DS9]
41 Art review, casually
42 Distress signal in "The Cage" [TOS]
47 Nancy who once loved Dr. McCoy
48 Acamarian killed by Riker in "The Vengeance Factor" [TNG]
50 Brock who played Sisko's father
52 Arton and Kurland
54 "Spock's ___" [TOS]
55 Heart line
56 Major Kira on *Deep Space Nine*
57 Human form assumed by the Caretaker
58 President's nay
59 Deltan killed by *V'Ger* in *The Motion Picture*
60 Medium killed by Redjac in "Wolf in the Fold" [TOS]
63 Perched
64 Liquidator Brunt's org.

Sam Bellotto Jr.

ACROSS

1 Unlike warp speed
5 Calamarain Berthold emissions in "Deja Q" [TNG]
9 "___ Women" [TOS]
14 Doctor's ___-resort in "Darkling" [VGR]
15 Busy as ___
16 Like the Void
17 Maple genus
18 Seven of ___
19 Damar's love interest in "Shadows and Symbols" [DS9]
20 *Star Trek* episode set on Elba II
23 Rabbit
24 "Expand ... or ___." (Ferengi rule)
25 Starfleet officer in "The Galileo Seven" [TOS]
28 One threw a drink in Sisko's face ("Dax" [DS9])
33 Bridge crew member of the *U.S.S. Voyager*
34 Unlike Rom's quarters
35 Durango airport code
36 Hint
37 Bajoran ___-sail vessel
38 ARA-scan detections
39 Wide shoe width
40 Conger or Ceti catcher
41 Commodore of Starbase 11 ("Court Martial" [TOS])
42 Archaeologist aboard the *U.S.S. Yamato* [TNG]
44 Tieran's foe in "Warlord" [VGR]
45 Half an antelope
46 Bashir's ___ ("Distant Voices" [DS9])
47 Space settlements in "Past Tense, Part I" [DS9]
55 "May the Great Bird of the Galaxy ___ on our planet.": Sulu
56 Morris in "Workforce, Part I" [VGR]
57 Certain
58 Jean-Luc Picard's aunt
59 Klingon battle cruiser in *The Motion Picture*
60 Jaret in "Prime Factors" [VGR]
61 Ferengi interloper in "The Perfect Mate" [TNG]
62 Odo's mentor Dr. ___ Pol
63 Dr. Helen in "Dagger of the Mind" [TOS]

DOWN

1 Prosecutor in "Court Martial" [TOS]
2 Scotty's lake
3 Bread spread
4 Celestial Temple, to Starfleet personnel
5 Vhnori thanatologist in "Emanations" [VGR]
6 Dwell
7 Longings
8 "Space ___" [TOS]
9 *Enterprise NX-01's* five-year ___
10 Becomes part of the Great Link
11 "Elementary, ___ Data" [TNG]
12 Ian Fleming villain
13 Layover
21 Terran explorer Vasco da ___
22 Chief Willoughby of Deep Space 9
25 Spiked the punch
26 *Enterprise* navigator in "The Cage" [TOS]
27 Ex-Yank Hank
28 Saavik's portrayer in *The Wrath of Khan*
29 ___ Admiral Bennett of Starfleet
30 Expression
31 *TOS* episode where Kirk fights the Gorn captain
32 Bre'ellians have blunt ones
34 Megan who was Noor in "The Outcast" [TNG]
37 Chakotay's lover in "Parallax" [VGR]
38 *U.S.S. Enterprise NCC-1701* officer [TOS]
40 Anyon ___
41 Prefix for conscious
43 Hars in *Insurrection*
44 Penny Johnson in "Homeward" [TNG]
46 Haliian artifact in "Aquiel" [TNG]
47 Sonant Starfleet exam
48 Took a travel pod
49 Earl in "Where Science Has Lease" [TNG]
50 Bilby in "Honor Among Thieves" [DS9]
51 ___ sapiens
52 ___-destruct sequence
53 Rubber ___ People ("Tattoo" [VGR])
54 "___ first; ask questions later." (Ferengi rule)

John M. Samson

ACROSS

1 "Loud ___ Whisper" [TNG]
4 Skidded
8 Unlike a *targ*
12 Barker and Perkins
13 Aunt who taught Picard home remedies
14 Wesley Crusher, once
15 "Master Melvin" of baseball
16 Barrett's credit in "The Cage" [TOS]
18 Sylvia's partner in "Catspaw" [TOS]
20 Main character of Vori war simulation in "Nemesis" [VGR]
21 See 7 Down
22 Dala's opponent in "Live Fast and Prosper" [VGR]
24 Award for *Deep Space Nine*
26 *Star Trek* creator
33 Rubicun III inhabitants in "Justice" [TNG]
34 "The Sound of ___ Voice" [DS9]
35 Murcia month
36 Matchstick game
37 Nebula studied in "Rightful Heir" [TNG]
40 Bounder
41 "This hair ___ is mine": Shak.
43 Infamous Barros ___
44 Had some Lorvan crackers
45 Barrett's role in *Star Trek*
50 Salesmen
51 What to use a magnesite-nitron tablet for
52 U.S. law-enforcement agency
55 Bajor's greatest hero Li
58 Assimilated Borg resister in "Unimatrix Zero" [VGR]
61 Barrett's role in *The Next Generation*
64 Quark's brother
65 Barrett
66 Duty-free
67 Conductor ___-Pekka Salonen
68 What David was to Carol and Jim
69 "___ Doctor" [ENT]
70 Romulan diplomat Caithlin in *The Final Frontier*

DOWN

1 "___ Time" [TOS]
2 Communications officer on *Enterprise NX-01*
3 Rain Robinson's profession in "Future's End" [VGR]
4 Space Lab in Logan, Utah
5 Soup plant
6 *Enterprise* navigator from Delta IV
7 With "The" and 21 Across, a *TNG* episode
8 ___ Ceti III, planet in "Conspiracy" [TNG]
9 Supplement: Abbr.
10 Encounter
11 Cut glass
13 Color of Acamarian brandy
14 Dilithium ___ hatch
17 Homeric poem in "Darmok" [TNG]
19 Golside or bolomite
23 Hibernating settlement in "The Thaw" [VGR]
25 Hankering
26 Ending for bio or cosmo
27 Keeler in "The City on the Edge of Forever" [TOS]
28 Dawn droplets
29 Power ___
30 Like Deep Space 9, twice
31 Give an adults-only label
32 Sing from Mont Blanc
37 "The ___ of Freedom" [TNG]
38 Big hand's dir. at 1:04
39 Ancient measure for joint of a king
42 Data doesn't need this
46 Vulcan doctor in "Suspicions" [TNG]
47 Tanagra, for example ("Damok" [TNG])
48 Name for a Suliban mothership
49 Narrow shoe width
52 ___ mater
53 Start of "Jabberwocky"
54 Collector Kivas in "The Most Toys" [TNG]
56 Put ___ in the water
57 Madrid miss: Abbr.
59 "Sub ___" [TNG]
60 Klingon battle cruiser destroyed by *V'Ger*
62 Alien prefix
63 An Argonaut pulled this

Sam Bellotto Jr.

ACROSS

1 Ancient name for Chekov's ancestral homeland
5 Prof. Seyetik in "Second Sight" [DS9]
10 Klingon ship in "A Matter of Honor" [TNG]
14 Back of the neck
15 Space hippie in "The Way to Eden" [TOS]
16 Jil ___, daughter of Gul Madred
17 Brothers' group
18 Commander of the *Kraxon* in "Defiant" [DS9]
19 Slender
20 Kirk's love in "City on the Edge of Forever" [TOS}
23 "___ program"
24 ___ Hugh Kelly of *Insurrection*
25 Coral island
27 *Enterprise* Stamp Committee founder
30 He played Chardis in "The Swarm" [VGR]
33 Money machine
36 Kind of tide
38 Ricky ___ Collins, boy in "Liaisons" [TNG]
39 Astronomer Robinson in "Future's End" [VGR]
41 ___ V, location of Farpoint Station
43 Hatae in "Rascals" [TNG]
44 Isok's brother in "Patterns of Force" [TOS]
46 Indian garment
47 Was victorious
48 Vorta in "Tacking Into the Wind" [DS9]
50 Zalkonian commander in "Transfigurations" [TNG]
53 Sticks in the mud
55 Starfleet Academy candidate in "Coming of Age" [TNG]
59 Security field subsystem ___
61 Kirk's old flame in *The Wrath of Khan*
64 Valet in "Our Man Bashir" [DS9]
66 She was Odala in "Distant Origin" [VGR]
67 Trail mix
68 Durken in "First Contact" [TNG]
69 Cargo ship in "Invasive Procedures" [DS9]
70 To be, to Caesar
71 Scalosian leader in "Wink of an Eye" [TOS]
72 ___ pod in "Liaisons" [TNG]
73 Light submachine gun

DOWN

1 Hungry
2 Dabo girl in "Captive Pursuit" [DS9]
3 He played a teenage Chakotay in "Tattoo" [VGR]
4 Kazon-Nistim leader in "Alliances" [VGR]
5 Kelli who played Rinna in "Favorite Sun" [VGR]
6 Dies ___ (Latin hymn)
7 "Life ___" [VGR]
8 ___ Gay, famed WW2 bomber
9 She was freed by Odo in "Vortex" [DS9]
10 Doctor who studied Odo
11 Kirk's old flame in "Court Martial" [TOS]
12 Mom's mom, familarly
13 It stopped the *Enterprise* in "Who Mourns for Adonis?"
21 *Enterprise* pronoun
22 Cross
26 Like Minos in "The Arsenal of Freedom" [TNG]
28 They're paid to Great Sages
29 Commander of the Vor'nak in "Sons and Daughters" [DS9]
31 Quark's cousin
32 7 in "A Taste of Armageddon" [TOS]
33 Shrinking sea
34 Visiting Talos IV, for one
35 Kirk's wife in "The Paradise Syndrome" [TOS]
37 Location in "Silent Enemy" [ENT]
40 Wife of the Tieran in "Warlord" [VGR]
42 Newton's ___ Theorem
45 Alaimo who played Gul Macet and Gul Dukat
49 Tidy up
51 *Parthas* ___ Yuta (vegetable dish) [TNG]
52 Solemn songs
54 He played Laxeth in "Investigations" [VGR]
56 Jared in "Devil's Duel" [TNG]
57 Christine Chapel was one
58 Colorado ski spot
59 Klingon battle cruiser destroyed by *V'Ger*
60 Starfleet Academy's ___ Squadron
62 Leave out
63 Singer Horne
65 "___ Our Yesterdays" [TOS]

Raymond Hamel

ACROSS

1 Odo can do this
6 "The Outrageous ___" [TNG]
11 Make lacy edges
14 In ___ (unborn)
15 Having two feet
16 "Falor's Journey" is one
17 Orellius ___ system
18 Lime-green beverage popular on Ferenginar
20 Janeway and Sisko, e.g.
22 Bajoran ___-sail vessel
23 It seized *Enterprise* in "Who Mourns for Adonis?" [TOS]
24 Gary Seven's cat
25 Gillespie in "Pen Pals" [TNG]
28 SSE or NNE: Abbr.
30 Thesaurus abbr.
32 Arguable
33 Norman in "Tapestry" [TNG]
34 Benjamin Sisko's second wife
38 Hawaiian menu fish
39 Vulcan mating instinct
41 Scotty's denial
42 Where Marritza said he taught in "Duet" [DS9]
44 Factory second: Abbr.
45 First name in spydom
46 Commanded
47 Cravat
48 Purim's month
49 Icheb's playmate in "Child's Play" [VGR]
52 Braxton's timeship in "Future's End" [VGR]
54 Chilled
56 *Enterprise NX-01* Captain Archer
60 Newcomer unacquainted with local ways
62 Word with space or shell
64 Extensive time frame
65 Species on Ledos in "Natural Law" [VGR]
66 Planet famous for amber-colored ale
67 Literary monogram
68 Mother of Ezri Dax, nee Tigan
69 Comes to a halt

DOWN

1 Tight-lipped
2 Of the ear
3 Western rockfish
4 "___ Motive" [DS9]
5 Creature in "The Devil in the Dark" [TOS]
6 Order headed by Enabran Tain
7 Brick-baking oven
8 Musical work
9 Spock's T-___ blood type: Abbr.
10 Excitements
11 Hyperspanner and magnaspanner, e.g.
12 U.S. statesman Stevenson
13 "___ of the Prophets" [DS9]
19 Ludugial gold ___ in "The Perfect Mate" [TNG]
21 36 Down is one
25 "___ Time" [TOS]
26 Taboo
27 Leader of the androgynous J'naii
29 *Starship Enterprise* overhaul
30 Race who believed Kentanna was Bajor
31 Tasha of *The Next Generation*
35 Telephathic Ullian historian in "Violations" [TNG]
36 Capt. Picard's XO
37 "___ of Hell" [VGR]
39 Rokeg blood ___
40 Destination in "Let That Be Your Last Battlefield" [TOS]
43 Name of ship Abaddon sells to Tom Paris
45 Episode where Mrs. Troi scours *Enterprise* for a mate
49 Carmel who played Harry Mudd
50 Enter Starfleet Academy
51 Appearances
53 Western Amerinds
55 Begrudge
56 Hole digger who joined Sybok's quest in *The Final Frontier*
57 Bajoran terrorist leader in "Ensign Ro" [TNG]
58 Carbon's "6": Abbr.
59 Tide type
61 "Had ___ hand to write this?": Shak.
63 TLC specialists

Sam Bellotto Jr.

ACROSS

1 Hallier in "Unity" [VGR]
5 Writer Bret
10 ___ Pran in "The Dogs of War" [DS9]
14 Form of Bajoran painting
15 Her name was Swahili
16 ___ Grey tea, a Picard favorite
17 Part of Trakor's Third Prophecy
18 Kara ___ in "Things Past" [DS9]
19 Aide to Gul Macet in "The Wounded" [TNG]
20 She married Benjamin Sisko
23 Disgraced Kazon in "Initiations" [VGR]
24 Captivate
25 River horse
27 Dr. Giger in "In the Cards" [DS9]
30 Navigator found in "The 37's" [VGR]
33 "The Naked ___" [TNG]
36 Arak'___, Jem'Hadar in "Hippocratic Oath" [DS9]
38 "___ Own Self" [TNG]
39 Vulcan death ___
41 Medication used in "Skin of Evil" [TNG]
43 Bajoran poet Akorem ___
44 Wormhole creator in "Rejoined" [DS9]
46 "The ___ Time" [TOS]
48 Bangkok-to-Hanoi dir.
49 Enaran in "Remember" [VGR]
51 Spock's father
53 Teller of fables
55 "Flash Gordon Conquers the Universe" was one
59 "The Mark of Gideon" [TOS] director Taylor
61 Shape-shifter
64 Jai ___
66 Eagle claw
67 Tactical officer in *Insurrection*
68 Sayana portrayer in "The Apple" [TOS]
69 Maquis in "Hunters" [VGR]
70 Solbor portrayer in " 'Til Death Do Us Part" [DS9]
71 Sales condition
72 Jones who played "Aquiel" [TNG]
73 Romulan operative played by Denise Crosby

DOWN

1 He was killed by the Vians in "The Empath" [TOS}
2 Atlantis Project location
3 Jeremiah ___ of "Suddenly Human" [TNG]
4 Before the deadline
5 Subservient humanoid in "The Nagus" [DS9]
6 Nautical greeting
7 Actress Lenska
8 Something to pledge
9 Make a gradual transition
10 Cassidy of "What Are Little Girls Made Of?" [TOS]
11 Talaxian war enemy
12 Cardassian Jil ___ in "Chain of Command, Part II" [TNG]
13 Tiburon on Deep Space 9
21 Cabbagehead
22 Data's cat
26 Younger brother to Kira Nerys
28 Nog portrayer Eisenberg
29 Dr. Kingsley of "Unnatural Selection" [TNG] et al.
31 David Opatoshu in "A Taste of Armageddon" [TOS]
32 Hawaiian goose
33 "___ tlhogh cha!" (Klingon divorce)
34 Terrorist in "Ensign Ro" [TNG]
35 Ambitious Bajoran leader
37 Governor of Peliar Zel in "The Host" [TNG]
40 French father
42 "Dramatis ___" [DS9]
45 Popular resort planet
47 Consider
50 ___ IV, planet in "We'll Always Have Paris" [TNG]
52 Phonetic spelling of the Klingon homeworld
54 Duranium ___ armor
56 Angry
57 Capt. Pike's predecessor
58 ___ apso (dog breed)
59 ___ Marie Hupp in "Galaxy's Child" [TNG]
60 Ethan Phillips role in "Acquisition" [ENT]
62 Ruck who played Capt. Harriman in *Generations*
63 Aching
65 Mirror *Enterprise* call letters

Raymond Hamel

ACROSS

1 He met with Pardek in "Unification" [TNG]
6 Cardassian Silaran killed by Kira
10 Use a dermal regenerator
14 Buenos Aires suburb
15 "Year of ___" [VGR]
16 George Takei's alma mater
17 Klingon adage: Part 1
20 Run ___ (owe)
21 Satellite launched in 1966
22 Ahn-woon, at times
23 Uhura's hairdo in *The Motion Picture*
25 Word form of "large"
27 Klingon adage: Part 2
34 DS9 first officer Kira
35 Wagner who played Krax
36 ___-mileage pit woofie
37 Actor's help
38 Evacuation-pod uses
42 Cardassian underground member in "Second Skin" [DS9]
43 What Tora Ziyal studied
44 Officer aboard *U.S.S. Okinawa* in "Paradise Lost" [DS9]
45 Arthur ___ Doyle
47 Translation of *Dal pagh jagh*
52 Akin to jejuno-
53 Where James T. Kirk was born
54 "___, the final frontier"
57 Tree on which Picard carved "A.F."
58 Gravitic sensor ___
62 Klingon observation
66 Seed integument
67 *The Next Generation* star
68 Jake's date in "It's Only a Paper Moon" [DS9]
69 He played Liria in "The Chute" [VGR]
70 "___ the picture"
71 Blue giant

DOWN

1 Greek gathering place
2 Pub measure
3 Kazon sect
4 Whiner
5 New Zealand parrot
6 ___ torpedoes
7 Antique autos
8 Stricken with the Phage
9 Common rebel org. Abbr.
10 Nebula where Ro defected
11 ___ Papa 607 ("The Arsenal of Freedom" [TNG])
12 Computer keys
13 Use a weapon as in "The Cage"
18 Vulcan *Pon* ___
19 Standard snowfall measure
24 Tuvok and Neelix do this in "Tuvix" [VGR]
25 Queue before q
26 Sickly chill
27 Atahualpa, notably
28 Kind of Borg transceivers
29 Mountain ridge
30 Voyager's destination in "Warlord" [VGR]
31 Cardassian scientist Belor in "Destiny" [DS9]
32 McDowell in *Generations*
33 She played Droxine in "The Cloud Minders" [TOS]
39 A few
40 ___-stasis units
41 Leaky freighter in "Final Mission" [TNG]
46 Sisko's favorite citrus fruits
48 DeBoer who played Ezri Dax
49 Robert at Appomattox
50 "Inter Arma Enim ___ Leges" [DS9]
51 Crewman in "The Galileo Seven" [TOS]
54 Wadi game chula level
55 Prefix for scope
56 Ilari doctor killed in "Warlord" [VGR]
57 French infinitive
59 Sunrise locale
60 ___ maneuver (bat'leth no-no)
61 ___-pei (Chinese fighting dog)
63 U.S. anti-ICBM plan
64 Quark's nephew
65 Boxing decision

Sam Bellotto Jr.

ACROSS

1 La Forge's name for Third of Five in "I, Borg" [TNG]
5 Gabosti dish prepared by Neelix in "Elogium" [VGR]
9 DNA and RNA, e.g.
14 Friend of Jadzia Dax in "You Are Cordially Invited" [DS9]
15 Ramscoop-like nodes in "Captive Pursuit" [DS9]
16 Cardassian planet in "Return to Grace" [DS9]
17 Go ballistic
18 Kind of admiral Bennett became
19 ___ Prime in "Remember" [VGR]
20 Star Trek pilot episode
22 First aired Star Trek episode (with "The")
24 Charles V's realm: Abbr.
25 "The ___ Is Cast" [DS9]
26 Humanoids in "When the Bough Breaks" [TNG]
30 He was Duras in "Sins of the Father" [TNG]
34 Heel-and-___ (race walker)
35 He drank poison in "The Quickening" [DS9]
37 Stackable item at Quark's
38 Vat
39 Zet's friend in "Renaissance Man" [VGR]
40 Android played by Ted Cassidy [TOS]
41 Alsia's monetary unit in "Rivals" [DS9]
43 1/20 latinum bar ("Body Parts" [DS9])
45 Burrow
46 Chief Edgar Willoughby's wife [DS9]
48 Federation captain killed in "Apocalypse Rising" [DS9]
50 Tongo in "The Way to Eden" [TOS]
51 "___ Pals" [TNG]
52 "The City on the Edge of ___" [TOS]
56 Star Trek epsiode set on Lyris VII
60 Enterprise-D destination in "A Matter of Time" [TNG]
61 Klingon Intelligence agent in "Visionary" [DS9]
63 "Inter ___ Enim Silent Leges" [DS9]
64 Third Talak'___ in "The Jem'Hadar" [DS9]
65 Klingon ___ of Heroes
66 Chlorinide container problem in "Ethics" [TNG]
67 Star Trek episode where the Metrons first appeared
68 Dax in "Playing God" [DS9]
69 Apollo's instrument

DOWN

1 Beverly in The Final Frontier
2 Beehive State
3 "Where No One Has ___ Before" [TNG]
4 Teri seen briefly in "The Outrageous Okona" [TNG]
5 He directed "The Corbomite Maneuver" [TOS]
6 Jumja tea source ("Crossover" [DS9])
7 Loseth in "Life Support" [DS9]
8 Tribbles are ___-blooded
9 Grem in "Second Skin" [DS9]
10 Captain Picard Day event in "The Pegasus" [TNG]
11 Brogger who was Orum in "Unity" [VGR]
12 Timicin's daughter in "Half a Life" [TNG]
13 What Kirk gave himself in "Plato's Stepchildren" [TOS]
21 Kind of lie-detector scan ("Ex Post Facto" [TNG])
23 Brinari leader in "Counterpoint" [VGR]
26 Loft
27 Crummy
28 Altec leader in "The Outrageous Okona" [TNG]
29 S.S. ___ Maria, personnel transport
30 Riker's teacher friend in "Inside Man" [VGR]
31 "Human ___" [VGR]
32 Gamma ___ IV in "The Last Outpost" [TNG]
33 Melthusian who discovered a rift ("Night Terrors" [TNG])
36 ___ Oscura Nebula
42 Klingon general who assassinated Emperor Reclaw
43 "This ___ of Paradise" [TOS]
44 Juice served at Ten-Forward Lounge
45 Brian in "Ethics" [TNG]
47 Federation starship in "Lessons" [TNG]
49 James Kirk's Butler, e.g.
52 Greek cheese
53 B'___ space in "The Raven" [VGR]
54 Stir up
55 Luma ___ , Kira Nerys pseudonym
56 Pick over
57 Klingon bird-of-___
58 Father of Kolax ("Prophecy" [VGR])
59 One was held for Captain Lisa Cusak on Deep Space 9
62 ___ kwon do

John M. Samson

ACROSS

1 Rocky crags
5 Water-collection pits
10 Top bean counter
13 Diva's solo
14 Blazing
15 Uru. neighbor
16 Security and Tactical Officer, *U.S.S. Voyager*
18 Odo's mentor in "The Alternate" [DS9]
19 Ensign Pavel aboard the *U.S.S. Enterprise*
20 Postured
21 Sicily's highest peak
22 Telepathic Ullian historian
24 Attack
26 Operators
29 *Delta Flyer* found it in "Thirty Days" [VGR]
31 Dolt
32 Tithe
33 Ocampa man in "Caretaker" [VGR]
36 Officer Lorenzo et al.
37 Chief Medical Officer, *Enterprise NCC-1701*
39 ___'q planet in "The Sword of Kahless" [DS9]
40 A Trill's brain has two
42 Ceti eel target in *The Wrath of Khan*
43 King mackerel
44 *TNG* episode where Picard was turned into a child
46 Suspira's ___ space station
47 He plays Geordi La Forge
48 Inexpensive swing
50 Brin ___ in "Things Past" [DS9]
51 ___ *Grande* (DS9 runabout)
53 She was Eleen in "Friday's Child" [TOS]
57 The Doctor on *Voyager* is one
58 Officer at Starbase 173 and Starbase 219
60 Copy
61 "Super!"
62 Italian wine center
63 Estonia, once: Abbr.
64 City of France
65 Lack

DOWN

1 Shaving powder
2 Word form of "straight"
3 Commander of the *U.S.S. Drake*
4 He was killed by Denevan neural parasites
5 Platoon NCO
6 Eskimo knives
7 Planetary system where Dr. Soong got married
8 Colyus' job in "Shadowplay" [DS9]
9 Son of 16 Across
10 Commanding officer, *Enterprise NX-01*
11 "Cold ___" [ENT]
12 Kazon sect led by Jal Razik
14 Nodes in Tosk's ship ("Captive Pursuit" [DS9])
17 Stark and Marshall
21 Heroic verse
23 Small portion
25 "A foolish thing was but ___": Shak.
26 Prussian cavalryman
27 Helm officer aboard *U.S.S. Enterprise*
28 Resident aboard *U.S.S. Enterprise-D* until 2367
30 Outshine
32 Handheld Starfleet sensor device
34 Atmosphere
35 David in "The Conscience of the King" [TOS]
37 Abbr. on an airline ticket
38 Brooks, Dorn, Visitor et al.
41 Voorhies in "Life Support" [DS9]
43 Unai aboard *Voyager*, e.g.
45 Kaverian tiger-bat, e.g.
46 Ronara Prime, DMZ ___
47 The Inheritors' forehead features
49 Like cuttlefish secretion
50 Tarkalean and Chiraltan
52 "___ Upon a Time" [VGR]
54 Episode where Odo and Lwaxana marry (with "The")
55 Cremona craft
56 Gatherers' foray
58 Thinking soc.
59 Satisfied sighs

Sam Bellotto Jr.

ACROSS

1 Weight-loss facilities
5 Curving pool shot
10 Ben Slack role in "Redemption" [TNG]
14 "It's supposed to ___, it's a phaser!": Quark
15 Contracted the Levodian flu
16 Ship-to-ship signal
17 Klingon ship in *The Motion Picture*
18 Gamma ___ II, planet in "The Vengeance Factor" [TNG]
19 Capture
20 One of Neelix's dishes
23 *Ch'Tang* helm officer in "Once More Unto the Breach" [DS9]
24 "Home ___" [TNG]
25 Long-time Daly costar
28 He played Yeggie in "Inside Man" [VGR]
32 Snack food made by Neelix
36 Sleep loudly
37 Anger
38 Tam
39 Cereal box info
40 Under, poetically
43 Dish from Neelix
47 Waitress on skates
49 She played the Borg queen [ST:FC]
50 Homeworld of "Elaan of Troyius" [TOS]
52 Bajoran faction fighting the Pagu
55 Treat from Neelix
59 Miramanee's father in "The Paradise Syndrome" [TOS]
61 Thief in "Resurrection" [DS9]
62 Ensign Chilton in "All Good Things..." [TNG]
63 Vulcan philosophy, for short
64 ___ Star Cluster in "Too Short a Season" [TNG]
65 Riker's *Imzadi*
66 Lunatic
67 Removed editorially
68 Door device

DOWN

1 Chase flies
2 Wild cats
3 "The Sheik of ___": 1921 hit
4 "___ Bedfellows" [DS9]
5 Brone player in "Nemesis" [VGR]
6 Puts on TV
7 Food ___
8 Big trucks
9 Wizard of Menlo Park
10 Annika Hansen portrayer Petersen
11 *VGR* episode (with "The")
12 "All systems go!"
13 Caustic cleaner
21 Before, to Brent Spiner
22 Neckwear not worn in the 23rd century
26 Of that sort
27 What the Hirogen do to prey
29 Italian leader Aldo
30 Delphi ___, world in "The Last Outpost" [TNG]
31 Kind of tide
32 Metallic element
33 Science specialty
34 Spock's pet
35 What Chakotay did in "The Boxer" [VGR]
41 Wrestler in "Tsunkatse" [VGR]
42 Black ___
44 Buster ___, sidekick to Capt. Proton
45 Sci-fi actor who married Shirley Temple
46 ___ Guarantee, part of the Federation Constitution
48 Like the Jem'Hadar skintone
51 Part of Riker's trombone
53 Music often sung by the EMH
54 Kar-___ Asteroid Belt
55 Kirk, Spock and McCoy, e.g.
56 Tuvok's daughter
57 Hawaiian honker
58 Error
59 Klingon ___ 'tal challenge
60 DS9 security chief

Raymond Hamel

ACROSS

1 ___-off (shortened)
5 Muldaur who played Dr. Pulaski
10 NY–LA direction
13 Olive genus
14 Elemspur Detention ___
15 Palindromic exclamation
16 Sisko's assignment before DS9
18 ___ *Grande* (DS9 runabout)
19 Thick soup
20 Road sign
21 Planet at war with Troyius
22 Contrite one
24 Jack Crusher's rank: Abbr.
26 Defender killed in "Nemesis" [VGR]
29 Response to "No you're not!"
31 Devonian ___
32 Loose
33 Tyree's enemy in "A Private Little War" [TOS]
37 *The Next Generation* premier episode locale
41 "Nor the Battle to the ___" [DS9]
42 Arctic explorer
43 Sea eagle
44 Spock's childhood pet
46 Leonard McCoy's nickname
48 Terrorist species in "The High Ground" [TNG]
50 "That's the humor ___": Shak.
52 Highlands hillside
53 Medicare's org.
55 Planet in Kobayashi Maru simulation
59 The Doctor on *Voyager* is one
60 *Voyager* premier episode locale
62 Russ who plays Tuvok
63 Mudd's women, e.g. [TOS]
64 Cartoonist Kelly
65 Black cuckoo
66 Sarava's Belmont win, for one
67 Mugato-like animals

DOWN

1 *Plomeek* ___
2 As well
3 Foiled assassin in *The Undiscovered Country*
4 Taresians' enemy in "Native Son" [VGR]
5 Roman goddess
6 Cornerback stats: Abbr.
7 Key rings?
8 Emulate Riva in "Loud as a Whisper" [TNG]
9 Heavenly altar
10 Qo'noS, for example
11 Romulan Tal ___ agent
12 Romances
14 Canadian tribe
17 "Son of ___!"
21 Pismire
23 Jeri on *Voyager*
25 Matador's cloak
26 They cry "foul!"
27 Smell ___ (suspect)
28 *Pon* ___ (Vulcan ritual)
30 Part of ESP
32 Ancient Bajoran craft
34 Jennifer who portrayed Kes
35 Data's brother
36 Dr. Mulhall and namesakes [TOS]
38 Sheriff's band
39 "___ penny ... hot cross buns"
40 Ensign Hoshi on *Enterprise*
45 Early starship weapons
46 Quinn who played David McCoy
47 Where Shatner first acted after college
48 Quark portrayer Shimerman
49 Planet where fever broke out in "Hollow Pursuits" [TNG]
51 Crazes
52 Sun ___ Niobe in "All Our Yesterdays" [TOS]
54 "One clover, and ___...": Dickinson
56 Take ___ (rest)
57 Thumb-twiddling
58 NASA *Enterprise* program: Abbr.
60 Houston college
61 21 Down is one

Sam Bellotto Jr.

ACROSS

1 Like Lt. Commander Shelby
6 Word with plane or length
11 *Defiant* conn officer in "Behind the Lines" [DS9]
14 Haile Selassie follower
15 "A Man ___" [DS9]
16 Muslim general
17 Felata ___ crisps
18 Lacerates
19 Japanese currency
20 Alpha Moon official in "The Host" [TNG]
22 Adm. Jameson's wife in "Too Short a Season" [TNG]
23 Crow's cry
24 Actress Pomers [*VGR*]
26 ___ capacitor, runabout device
29 Troi pronoun
31 Woman in "Violations" [TNG]
32 Hunter of Lokai in "Let That Be Your Last Battlefield" [TOS]
34 All-night party
36 Bajoran in "Destiny" [DS9]
40 "Friendship One" woman [VGR]
41 Feature of Vulcan ears
43 Brother of Kira Nerys
44 "___ of Flux" [VGR]
46 Research ship lost in "Hero Worship" [TNG]
47 Katarina of "Haven" [TNG]
48 Planet in "Whom Gods Destroy" [TOS]
50 Greek vowel
52 Millions of years
53 Trill, for one
57 Many, many mins.
59 Rapier
60 Garth in "Whom Gods Destroy" [TOS]
65 Quark's younger sib
66 Kamin's wife in "The Inner Light" [TNG]
67 Maugham's Miss Thompson
68 Mouths, zoologically
69 ___ Alpha, class 9 pulsar
70 Bender in "Manhunt" [TNG]
71 Nimoy song "Visit to a ___ Planet"
72 Minimal
73 Telepathic ambassador in "Man of the People" [TNG]

DOWN

1 ___'tan, Klingon in "Barge of the Dead" [VGR]
2 ___ IV, world in "The Survivor" [TNG]
3 Member of Tuvok's family
4 Like Tuvok
5 Genome Colony member in "The Masterpiece Society" [TNG]
6 She played Langor in "Symbiosis" [TNG]
7 Butter substitutes
8 "The ___ of the King" [TOS]
9 Like llamas
10 "Tapestry" [TNG] director Landau
11 Turkana IV leader in "Legacy" [TNG]
12 V'Shar or Arne Darvin
13 Dr. Wallace in "The Deadly Years" [TOS]
21 Insignificant person
22 Gul Danar's warship in "Past Prologue" [DS9]
25 Young who played Morka in "Visionary" [DS9]
26 Flows out
27 Sassy
28 She was attacked by *V'Ger*
30 Criminal in "The Passenger" [DS9]
33 *U.S.S. Ulysses* captain in "The Adversary" [DS9]
35 Sigma Draconis ___ in "Spock's Brain" [TOS]
37 Odo portrayer Auberjonois
38 Ferengi thief in "Shadowplay" [DS9]
39 War leader in "A Taste of Armageddon" [TOS]
42 "___ Death" [DS9]
45 Gunfighter Hollander in "A Fistful of Datas" [TNG]
49 ___ freighter in "Sons of Mogh" [DS9]
51 Odo fell for her in "A Simple Investigation" [DS9]
53 Dejaren's home planet ("Revulsion" [VGR])
54 Bajoran midwife in "The Begotten" [DS9]
55 Enabran Tain's enemy ("In Purgatory's Shadow" [DS9])
56 Mortise companion
58 "And the Children ___ Lead" [TOS]
61 Hiding place of uniforms in *The Undiscovered Country*
62 Minn. neighbor
63 Verdi opera set in Egypt
64 Ten Tribes leader in "Friday's Child" [TOS]
66 Lauter and Begley

Raymond Hamel

ACROSS

1 Barrel
5 Dabo and *kal-toh*
10 Par Lenor's assistant [TNG]
13 "___ of Fear" [TNG]
15 Speedskater Ohno
16 ___-Magnon man
17 Kirk and Picard joined forces to stop him
19 Hospital areas
20 Crater who once loved Leonard McCoy
21 Pig's digs
22 Cloning chains
23 Schools of whales
25 Sporty scarf
27 Beaming
30 Table in which element 247 does not appear
33 Brown in "Prophecy" [VGR]
34 "He ___ sell ice on Rura Penthe" (Klingon proverb)
35 Persephone's love
37 Teachers' org.
38 Angela in "Shore Leave" [TOS]
40 Yorkshire river
41 Ski
43 ER personnel
44 Grayish purple
45 Like Ferengi for latinum
47 Composer Bernstein
48 News summary
49 Root beer, e.g.
51 Exploding peril in *Generations*
53 Shootist's org.
55 Choreographer De Mille
58 "Surprise!"
59 Social worker in "The City on the Edge of Forever" [TOS]
62 Equip with phasers
63 Star in "The Child" [TNG]
64 "Heart of ___" [DS9]
65 MPAA ratings
66 Ensign on the *Enterprise-D* under Picard
67 Jaxa in "Lower Decks" [TNG]

DOWN

1 TV tube
2 Captain Braxton's timeship
3 Casa room
4 Khitomer massacre victim
5 Kind of nebula
6 G.I. addresses
7 Kirk's cannon in "Arena" [TOS]
8 Humanoid species in "Melora" [DS9]
9 Worf, to Mogh
10 Extradimensional domain [TNG, VGR]
11 Jil in "Chain of Command, Part 1" [TNG]
12 "Profit and ___" [DS9]
14 Largest parrot
18 Servant of Falstaff
22 Extinct Earth bird
24 Box
26 ___ Factor 1
27 Sheaf bristles
28 ___-Roman wrestling
29 *Enterprise-D* warp engine designer
31 ___ nous (confidentially)
32 *Odyssey* enchantress
34 Orellius siren in "Paradise" [DS9]
36 Sybo, for one ("Wolf in the Fold" [TOS])
38 Light speed, for short
39 Unaffiliated pols: Abbr.
42 Kind of friendly
44 Bajor and Betazed
46 ___ wine (Bajoran beverage)
47 Borders
50 Mighty tree
51 Wadi chula term
52 Piglike Klingon animal
54 Suit to ___
56 *The Time Machine* race
57 E-mailed
59 A Vulcan's is pointed
60 Harvard business mag
61 ___ Speedwagon

Sam Bellotto Jr.

ACROSS

1 ___-lash, fruit in "Hard Time" [DS9]
5 Morris in "One Small Step" [VGR]
9 Ill-temper
14 ___ of Audiences in "Return of the Archons" [TOS]
15 Doctor's wife in "Endgame, Part I" [VGR]
16 Star Wesley Crusher sees in "The Child" [TNG]
17 Wings
18 Jil in "Chain of Command, Part I" [TNG]
19 Cardassian outpost in "Return to Grace" [DS9]
20 Klingon ritual shaming
23 Cravat
24 Bemonite, e.g. ("Once Upon a Time" [VGR])
25 Will ___, Worf's role in "Qpid" [TNG]
29 Volcano ascended by Kahless the Unforgettable
33 ___ VII, planet in "The Chute" [VGR]
34 Security officer in "Work Force" [VGR]
36 "___-Q" [TNG]
37 She, in Rio
38 Early 21st-century Terran music
39 Data's "grandfather" Dr. Graves
40 Garak in "Empok Nor" [DS9]
42 Drug given to Natasha Yar in "Skin of Evil" [TNG]
44 Ruck in *Generations*
45 Skunk
47 Saviola who was Kai Opaka in "Emissary" [DS9]
49 Sound from Dr. Crusher in 36 Across
50 "___ the Cause" [DS9]
51 *TNG* episode where Worf accepted 20 Across
60 Above a whisper
61 Alfarian ___ pasta
62 Jean-Luc Picard's nephew
63 Rhone tributary
64 Voval's human alias in "Liaisons" [TNG]
65 Command module in "One Small Step" [VGR]
66 Dr. Quaice in "Remember Me" [TNG]
67 Bajoran hologram in "Flesh and Blood, Part I" [VGR]
68 Father of Worf and Kurn

DOWN

1 Allen who was Jono in "Suddenly Human" [TNG]
2 Mintakan hunter in "Who Watches the Watchers?" [TNG]
3 Neighboring planet of Troyius [TOS]
4 Earhart's abandoned Lockheed ___ plane in "The 37's" [VGR]
5 Orange Vulcan soup
6 Damage
7 Concerning
8 Bajoran poet Akorem in "Accession" [DS9]
9 Underground race in "Blood Fever" [VGR]
10 "I ___. I am not a merry man!": Worf ("Qpid" [TNG])
11 Crucifix letters
12 ___'Zuma, Jem'Hadar soldier in "Hippocratic Oath" [DS9]
13 Israel's first UN delegate
21 Kolaish spice ___
22 He's Worf
25 Woolly creatures of Tarkalia
26 Miles O'Brien plays one
27 To no ___ (fruitlessly)
28 Cards at a reading
29 Rayna in "Requiem For Methuselah" [TOS]
30 Joined species in "Rejoined" [DS9]
31 Acoustic
32 Kerrie who's Devos in "The High Ground" [TNG]
35 Galek in "Booby Trap" [TNG]
41 "The ___ of a Man" [TNG]
42 She was Sonya in "Q Who?" [TNG]
43 Vhnori city in "Emanations" [VGR]
44 Kirk rode one in *The Motion Picture*
46 Rakhari fugitive in "Vortex" [DS9]
48 Bird once hunted by Maori
51 Uttered
52 Anagram name of Lisa
53 Doctor Helen in "Dagger of the Mind" [TOS]
54 Siamese
55 Emergency ___ actuator ("Disaster" [TNG])
56 Mozart's "___ kleine Nachtmusik"
57 "Fallen ___" [ENT]
58 Zeon rebel in "Patterns of Force" [TOS]
59 Tieran's military advisor in "Warlord" [VGR]

John M. Samson

ACROSS

1 Scoundrel
5 Tuvok's wife
9 F-16, for one
12 Painted metalware
13 Mist
14 Maquis unit
15 Suffix for Saturn
16 Curtis of aviation
17 Roughly
18 Sisko's illusion in "If Wishes Were Horses" [DS9]
20 More underhanded
21 Wormhole particle
22 Mintakan hunter in "Who Watches the Watchers?" [TNG]
24 Vulcan ___ philosophy
27 Dr. Lester in "Turnabout Intruder" [TOS]
31 *Voyager* episode featuring Qatai
35 Ankara native
37 De France and du Diable
38 O'Brien's illusion in "If Wishes Were Horses" [DS9]
41 Kirghizian range
42 Chits
43 ___ *of Two Cities*: Dickens
44 Maintenance corridor on Deep Space 9
46 She plays Sato on *Enterprise*
48 Suffix for disk
50 Protection
54 Scenic Da Vinci ___ in "Second Sight" [DS9]
57 Bashir's illusion in "If Wishes Were Horses" [DS9]
61 Matinee follower
62 Copycat's words
63 Stone suffix
64 Symbiont Dax's host after Jadzia
65 Anton Karidian, for one
66 Hydroxyl compound
67 Tip
68 Romulan ___ Empire
69 El ___ (Pacific current)

DOWN

1 Use a *d'k tahg*
2 "Wild Earth" poet Padraic
3 Krige who played the Borg queen
4 Avianoid aliens have them
5 A long voyage
6 Mountain lion
7 Internet letter
8 German rocketeer Willy
9 Ryan on *Voyager*
10 More
11 Tiburon who surveyed Torga IV [DS9]
13 Majel Barrett's hair color as Nurse Chapel
14 Carmen Davila in "Silicon Avatar," e.g. [TNG]
19 Idaho's largest city
20 Reggae predecessor
23 H-M links
25 "Make ___": Picard
26 Jokester
28 Chase of "Now, Voyager"
29 Enclose the atrium
30 Anglo-Saxon menial
31 Imp
32 Pip
33 Martia in *The Undiscovered Country*
34 Lieutenant cited by Kirk in "Space Seed" [TOS]
36 Tropical resort planet in "Captain's Holiday" [TNG]
39 Rhythmic swing
40 George seen in "Flashback" [VGR]
45 UFO pilots
47 Tarcassian ___ beast
49 Get rid of a warp core, say
51 Picard's old archaeology professor
52 ___ Star Cluster
53 Silenced
54 Feudal estate
55 Logging tool
56 Brent Spiner role
58 "___ boy!"
59 "The Royale" has a revolving one [TNG]
60 Lwaxana Troi's aide before Mr. Homn ("Haven" [TNG])
62 Moms

Sam Bellotto Jr.

ACROSS

1 Daddies
6 "Encore!"
10 Seven player
14 Bajoran scientist Belor in "Destiny" [DS9]
15 Baldwin in *The Hunt for Red October*
16 Duran'___, Jem'Hadar in "One Little Ship" [DS9]
17 Silver blood, e.g. ("Demon" [VGR])
18 Ops officer in "Redemption, Part 1" [TNG]
19 "Whom ___ Destroy" [TOS]
20 *VGR* episode with Neelix disguised as a Ferengi
23 Lal, to Lore
24 "Tinker, Tenor, Doctor, ___" [VGR]
25 Singer Peeples
28 Martial ___
31 "___ Sight" [DS9]
33 Kirk is disguised as a Romulan in "The ___ Incident" [TOS]
38 Klingon agent Darvin in "The Trouble With Tribbles" [TOS]
39 *Enterprise NX-01* armory officer [ENT]
40 Sound booster
41 Part of a bridal attire
42 Cuba, e.g.
43 Sisko masqueraded as a Klingon in "___ Rising" [DS9]
46 Klingon revived from suspended animation in "The Emissary"
48 "By Any Other ___" [TOS]
49 "All I ___ is a tall ship": Kirk
50 ___'Rok, energy creature in "The Storyteller" [DS9]
52 *DS9* star Brooks
56 *DS9* episode with Kira disguised as a Breen
60 Prison administrator in "Hard Time" [TNG]
63 Jazz singer James
64 Aldean leader in "When the Bough Breaks" [TNG]
65 Samoan dancer at the Dax engagement party
66 Romulan defector in "Face of the Enemy" [TNG]
67 Start of the Spanish calendar
68 ___ Byron in "Darkling" [VGR]
69 Klingon mercenary in "Invasive Procedures" [DS9]
70 Picard's paramour in "Lessons" [TNG]

DOWN

1 Ktarian chocolate ___
2 "Tears of the Prophets" [DS9] director Kroeker
3 Russian tsar
4 Biscotti flavoring
5 Spot for a motorcycle passenger
6 Vengeful xenologist in "Silicon Avatar" [TNG]
7 Bread spread
8 Coral constructions
9 Solar ___
10 Starfleet legal officers: Abbr.
11 Civilization on Rubicun III in "Justice" [TNG]
12 Tongo ___, ambassador's son in "The Way to Eden" [TOS]
13 U.S. tax agency
21 Criminal
22 Ferengi in "Civil Defense" [DS9]
25 Medication used in "Skin of Evil" [TNG]
26 First Electorine in "Haven" [TNG]
27 Jean-Luc Picard's aunt
29 "The Man ___" [TOS]
30 Dr. Van Gelder in "Dagger of the Mind" [TOS]
32 Guinea pig
33 Commander Benteen in "Homefront" [DS9]
34 Hornets' homes
35 Vetor officer in "Journey's End" [TNG]
36 Wax-coated cheese
37 Humane org.
43 Starfleet training ground
44 Klingon battle cruiser in *The Motion Picture*
45 Pried
47 ___ recoupler, engineering tool
51 Petrol measure
53 Ktarian operative Jol
54 Michael in "The Naked Now" [TNG]
55 "Mr. Spock, ___ a stubborn man!": Kirk
56 Telepathic historian in "Violations" [TNG]
57 Editorial comment
58 Roman "Censor"
59 Element #10
60 He had a brief affair with Troi in "The Price" [TNG]
61 He played Chang in "Coming of Age" [TNG]
62 Likewise not

Raymond Hamel

ACROSS

1 Vulcans embrace this
6 Grasslands
10 ___ cat (Bajoran animal)
14 Like Finnegan in "Shore Leave" [TOS]
15 Commedia dell'___
16 Klingon ___ history
17 Quadrant in which *U.S.S. Voyager* got lost
18 Janeway portrayer Mulgrew
19 Emotion explored in "QPid" [TNG]
20 System that includes Earth
21 Krazy of comics
23 Negatively charged
25 Word form of "mouth"
26 ___ salad (a favorite of Chakotay)
27 Wrath
30 Tactical Officer on the *U.S.S. Voyager*
32 Trianic-based energy beings in "Heroes and Demons" [VGR]
36 Jake Sisko's dad
38 Acclamation for Zapata
39 Set at ease
40 Publishers' org.
42 Dr. Noel in "Dagger of the Mind" [TOS]
43 Be a bookworm
44 State of maximum readiness on Federation vessels
46 Commandeer
48 Country estate
49 Method: Abbr.
50 Falls in Zaire
52 Bajoran composer Jolan
53 Capt. Janeway's ship
56 Suffix for element
57 Sound like Spot
60 Copied
61 Worf has one on his arm
63 Australian "teddy bear"
65 Stiff hair
66 George Takei role
67 Gamma Quadrant ternary star in "Emissary" [DS9]
68 Feminine ending
69 Sugar suffixes
70 Rafalian ___ in "Crossfire" [DS9]

DOWN

1 They're on top of things
2 Cream-filled cookie
3 Federation historian who corrupted the culture of Ekos
4 It's right after left
5 First Officer on the *U.S.S. Voyager*
6 Population center bombed by Open Sky in "The Chute" [VGR]
7 Stretch of time
8 Fire phasers at
9 "Hear no evil, ___ evil ..."
10 Janeway's Gothic work in "Cathexis" [VGR]
11 Eisenberg of Nog fame
12 Sitarist Shankar
13 Stage actor Clunes
22 Calla lily
24 Bother
27 Steel girders
28 Gen. at Gettysburg
29 Chou ___
31 Bajoran featured in "Accession" [DS9]
33 DS9 Chief of Operations O'Brien
34 Brooks who plays Captain Sisko
35 Storms
37 DS9 Science Officer
41 Wesley and Picard's destination in "Final Mission" [TNG]
42 Operations Officer on the *U.S.S. Voyager*
45 Hatch on a starship
47 Robin Hood's land: Abbr.
48 Kirk's son David
51 Bas-relief material
53 Like the universe
54 Phone abbr.
55 Abominable Snowman
57 *Kobayashi* ___ scenario
58 Planet at war with Troyius
59 Abate
62 Trakian brew
64 DS9 Promenade Security Officer

Sam Bellotto Jr.

ACROSS

1 ___ factor
5 Move down the Z axis
9 Degebian mountain ___
13 Aviation pioneer Sikorsky
14 Berne river
15 Jal ___, Kazon-Pommar contact in "Alliances" [VGR]
16 "___ the Winner" ("Bread and Circuses" [TOS])
17 Doran's father in "Sons and Daughters" [DS9]
18 Dr. Bashir's mother
19 Klingon interferer in "Friday's Child" [TOS]
20 Object of desire for the creature in 25 Across
22 Dr. Arridor in "False Profits" [VGR]
24 Record keeper in "Who Watches the Watchers?" [TNG]
25 TOS episode with a shapeshifting creature
30 Adventurous archaeologist in "Captain's Holiday" [TNG]
34 Hekaran scientist in "Force of Nature" [TNG]
35 "Threshold" [VGR] meas.
36 Astronaut Jemison
37 Federation mediator in "The Host" [TNG]
38 Rundown
40 Of the flock
41 Borg virus creator in "Infinite Regress" [VGR]
42 Data's poem "___ to Spot"
43 Aide to Ambasssador Ves Alkar in "Man of the People" [TNG]
44 Signs off
46 Poisonous plant in 25 Across
49 "Who ___ to argue with history?": Kirk
51 ___-jytsu, martial arts form mastered by Riker
52 Emotional plant in 25 Across
57 "Thine Own ___" [TNG]
61 Android series in "I, Mudd" [TOS]
62 Dax played by Nicole deBoer
63 Deltan navigator in The Motion Picture
64 Bathroom fixture
65 Underground member in "Patterns of Force" [TOS]
66 Support a crook
67 Klingon ship in The Motion Picture
68 NX-01 communications officer [ENT]
69 Bajoran cleric in "Sons and Daughters" [DS9]

DOWN

1 "___ of an Eye" [TOS]
2 Goran'___ in "Hippocratic Oath" [DS9]
3 Tomato variety
4 Amb. Krajensky in "The Adversary" [DS9]
5 B'elanna Torres portrayer
6 U.S.S. Antares captain in "Charlie X" [TOS]
7 Kind of history
8 Saucy
9 Planet in "Basics, Part I" [VGR]
10 River into the Caspian Sea
11 Tennis great Arthur
12 Ferengi captain in "The Last Outpost" [TNG]
15 Child actor Mowry in "Innocence" [VGR]
21 Collect liquid
23 Meteorologist Moseley in "A Matter of Time" [TNG]
25 Treasure collection
26 Starfleet admiral played by John Hancock
27 Emissions from collapsing protostars
28 Kolaati participant in "Fair Trade" [VGR]
29 U.S. medical org.

31 Security officer killed by Garak in "Empok Nor" [DS9]
32 He played Nogami in "The 37's" [VGR]
33 Mauna Apgar player in "A Matter of Perspective" [TNG]
38 She played Ulani Belor in "Destiny" [DS9]
39 Humanoid race in "Justice" [TNG]
40 Virus in "If Wishes Were Horses" [DS9]
43 Short punch
45 Enterprise-D module
47 Attic room
48 Deep reddish blue
50 Romulan defector in 2369 [TNG]
52 Ali ___
53 ___ Garak
54 Verdi opera
55 Exclamations of wonder
56 Favorite dish of Jadzia Dax
58 Planet in "Whom Gods Destroy" [TOS]
59 Kes player
60 Destiny

Raymond Hamel

ACROSS

1 Communications Officer on *Enterprise*
5 Geordi La Forge food favorite
10 Noun suffix
14 Part of XO: Abbr.
15 "___ of Troyius" [TOS]
16 Bikini island
17 Aloe ___
18 Coalition on Natasha Yar's home planet
19 Turn aside
20 Cardassian tailor on Deep Space 9
22 "I" problem
23 *Fal-tor-*___ (Spock's rebirth)
24 Neelix is one
28 Do like Bareil Antos (mirror)
31 Alfre Woodard in *First Contact*
32 Pinch a pinscher
34 Denizens of Mariposa or Aldea
38 Buenos Aires locale: Abbr.
39 Chief Engineer McDougal in "The Naked Now" [TNG]
41 Cartoonist Gardner
42 Planet with two warring nations in "Attached" [TNG]
45 "Cause and ___" [TNG]
48 Diplomacy
49 "All humans look ___ to Ferengi": Quark
50 Captain Archer on *Enterprise*
54 Number of Kirks in "The Enemy Within" [TOS]
55 English actress Mary
56 Location of Starfleet facility in "The Man Trap" [TOS]
61 Lt. Romaine in "The Lights of Zetar" [TOS]
63 He recruited Kira at age 12
64 Container weight
65 Delights
66 Middle, in law
67 Asteroid watched by NEAR
68 Saturn ring "handle"
69 Source of Drakian syrup
70 Blow a gasket

DOWN

1 Golfer Ballesteros
2 Skating jump
3 She played Roberta in "Assignment Earth" [TOS]
4 Kes, for example
5 Pie in "Prime Factors" [VGR]
6 Like horse Pegasus
7 Egyptian Peace Nobelist
8 Planet known for its species of sheep
9 French donkey
10 Response: Abbr.
11 Sulu portrayer
12 "The ___ Directive" [VGR]
13 Romulan who intended to destroy DS9 in "Visionary"
21 Formal affair
25 Like the J'naii ("The Outcast" [TNG])
26 Boxing great
27 Affair of 1778
28 Mount Rushmore locale: Abbr.
29 Satie's assistant in "The Drumhead" [TNG]
30 What the Horta protected in "The Devil in the Dark" [TOS]
33 Kind of technician in "Wolf in the Fold" [TOS]
34 Computer monitor
35 "... ___ saw Elba"
36 Location of Spock's famous pinch
37 Fill to the brim
40 Klingon bird-of-prey, usually
43 U.S. school org.
44 Bulgallian ___
46 Curry favor
47 Holograph in "Once Upon a Time" [VGR]
50 Deep Space 9 Promenade stick candy
51 Syndicate in "A Simple Investigation" [DS9]
52 Kira of Deep Space 9
53 Like King Hrothgar
54 *DS9* episode "___ Orphan"
57 Robert Picard's son
58 ___ cat
59 "Old ___ Boots" (Riker's ancestor Thaddius)
60 It has no sleeves
62 Cool ___ cucumber
63 Total: Abbr.

Sam Bellotto Jr.

ACROSS

1 Lycia in "Samaritan Snare" [TNG]
5 Dr. Kingsley in "Unnatural Selection" [TNG]
9 Dax host in "Nor the Battle to the Strong" [DS9]
14 Girl in "Chain of Command, Part II" [TNG]
15 Juliana Tainer's husband ("Inheritance" [TNG])
16 Goofed
17 Tieran's physician in "Warlord" [VGR]
18 Captain Braxton's Federation timeship
19 Ya'Seem discoverer in "The Chase" [TNG]
20 *Voyager* episode that preceded "Prey"
22 "All Our Yesterdays" [TOS] author
24 Bajoran ___ of Time
25 Where a *bat'leth* is carried ("Reunion" [TNG])
26 Bajoran ___ of Ministries
30 Pah-___, Bajoran Prophets' enemies ("The Reckoning" [DS9])
34 Data's "brother"
35 O'Grady of song
37 He was Keevan in "Rocks and Shoals" [DS9]
38 The Altar constellation
39 Penthor-___ in "The Vengeance Factor" [TNG]
40 Operated
41 Federation President Jaresh-___ ("Homefront" [DS9])
43 Sector in "Face of the Enemy" [TNG]
45 Spiritual leader in "Rapture" [DS9]
46 Parinisti disease in "Heroes and Demons" [VGR]
48 Wife of Lutan in "Code of Honor" [TNG]
50 Telek R'___ in "Eye of the Needle" [VGR]
51 First name of 14 Across
52 Maquis in "The Maquis, Part I" [DS9]
56 Poet Sean in "Fair Haven" [VGR]
60 Overplay the role
61 Klingon prisoner in "Birthright, Part I" [TNG]
63 Net sport in "A Man Alone" [DS9]
64 "___ Defense" [DS9]
65 Kang's wife in "Day of the Dove" [TOS]
66 Old ___ in "Catspaw" [TOS]
67 Redjac's victim in "Wolf in the Fold" [TOS]
68 Nog portrayer Eisenberg
69 *Apollo II* launcher

DOWN

1 Dr. Hippocrates in "Our Man Bashir" [DS9]
2 Delphi ___, planetary system in "The Last Outpost" [TNG]
3 Quark's uncle
4 The Doctor named him in "The Void" [VGR]
5 Herschel who played 41 Across
6 Command module in "One Small Step" [VGR]
7 Vantika in "The Passenger" [DS9]
8 She kissed Picard in "Liaisons" [TNG]
9 *Escort*-class starship
10 Federation ship in "The Ensigns of Command" [TNG]
11 Furors
12 Pool-table top
13 Run in neutral
21 She was Liva in "Man of the People" [TNG]
23 Like eisilium ("Breaking the Ice" [ENT])
26 Something to stake
27 Picard's creative-writing teacher ("The Game" [TNG])
28 Hatil's wife in "Emanations" [VGR]
29 Ornaran in "Symbiosis" [TNG]

30 He was Vagh in "The Mind's Eye" [TNG]
31 Number of moons orbiting 57 Down
32 He was Berel in "First Contact" [TNG]
33 Yemeni port
36 Varis in "The Storyteller" [DS9]
42 Dermal ___ sealant ("Parturition" [VGR])
43 He was Kellan in "Dreadnought" [VGR]
44 Ro Laren or 45 Across, e.g.
45 Deputy Fuhrer on Ekos in "Patterns of Force" [TOS]
47 "___ Among Us" [TNG]
49 Apparatus
52 Children of the Sun, for one
53 Mideast prince
54 Tholl in "Allegiance" [TOS]
55 2001 award given Roxann Dawson
56 Tribal elder in "The Paradise Syndrome" [TOS]
57 Delta ___ IV, planet in "The Survivors" [TNG]
58 Very, in France
59 *Voyager* crewman in "Repression" [VGR]
62 Kazlon-Ogla warrior in "Initiations" [VGR]

John M. Samson

ACROSS

1 When erosene winds blow on Alastria
6 Klingon ship on which Riker briefly served
10 Prof.'s aides
13 N Brazil territory
14 Deltan navigator who served under Capt. Kirk
15 Ilari commander in "Warlord" [VGR]
16 Snub
17 "Just Married" sign accompaniments
18 K–12
19 ___ Draconis VI in "Spock's Brain" [TOS]
21 Capt. Kirk's portrayer
23 Capt. Benjamin Sisko, to Bajorans
26 Salinger who was Lupaza [DS9]
27 Commander of the *U.S.S. Drake* killed at Minos
28 Tauvid Rem in "A Simple Investigation," e.g. [TNG]
31 McKinley's first lady
32 Quint of the Caldos colony in "Sub Rosa" [TNG]
33 W Samoan capital
37 Investigator in "A Matter of Perspective" [TNG]
39 Black-and-white criminal sought by Bele
41 Boys
42 First-rate
43 "You ___ Cordially Invited ..." [DS9]
44 Suffix for bishop
45 Matriarchal race that settled on Draylon II
49 Sicilian volcano
50 Commenced
53 *Enterprise* or *Voyager*
55 Riker's first starship assignment
58 Japanese lyric verse
59 Lab gel
60 Where Rain Robinson worked in "Future's End" [VGR]
62 Sanctuary District resident in "Past Tense" [DS9]
65 Vulgar
66 Scots name
67 On-line letter
68 Baseball stat
69 Trekkies, e.g.
70 Pulsar in "Allegiance" [TNG]

DOWN

1 H.S.H., à la française
2 Ballpark figure
3 One stabbed a young Picard in the heart
4 Ascend
5 Hunger signs
6 ___ Maneuver
7 Pie-mode links
8 Snares
9 Corned-beef dish for Miles O'Brien
10 Bajoran temple preacher [DS9]
11 Blanched
12 English county
15 ___ imaging scan in "The Passenger" [Ds9]
20 Merry month in Paris
22 Dental org.
23 Starfleet Officer Benteen in "Paradise Lost" [DS9]
24 Troglyte Disrupter in "The Cloud Minders" [TOS]
25 Baseball team praised by Vin in "Past Tense, Part II" [DS9]
29 20th-century teachers' gp.
30 "Big Daddy" Amin
34 Like B'Elanna Torres
35 Star cluster in "Too Short a Season" [TNG]
36 Tin Pan Alley org.
38 Maiden name of Jean-Luc Picard's mother
39 Burmese gibbon
40 Officer on *U.S.S. Okinawa* in "Paradise Lost" [TNG]
46 Ocampan crewmember on *Voyager*
47 *TNG* episode in which Worf attempts ritual Klingon suicide
48 Battery size
49 Anorak wearer
50 "... and behold ___ horse": Rev. 6:8
51 Beta III native immune from absorption into the Body
52 Head Nurse Alyssa aboard *U.S.S. Enterprise* [TNG]
54 Star system visited in "Broken Bow" [ENT]
56 John Christopher's service in "Tomorrow Is Yesterday" [TOS]
57 Natasha Yar's daughter
61 *U.S.S. Enterprise-D* ___-Forward lounge
63 "Ferd'nand" cartoonist
64 Guido's note

Sam Bellotto Jr.

ACROSS

1 Varis ___ in "The Storyteller" [DS9]
4 Fanatical Borg in "Descent" [TNG]
10 Nancy Crater's nickname for McCoy in "The Man Trap" [TOS]
14 Stem bolt buyer in "Prophet Motive" [DS9]
15 Worf's ship in "Redemption, Part I" [TNG]
16 Hecht of "A Matter of Perspective" [TNG]
17 *Maj* ___, Klingon for "good night"
18 More slippery
19 Somewhat
20 Phrase Data learned in "Hide and Q" [TNG]
23 Summer back home, to Picard
24 Ensign Jaxa in "Lower Decks" [TNG]
25 Ensign Renlay in "The Fight" [VGR]
27 Hannah in "The Masterpiece Society" [TNG]
32 Invitation to a hitchhiker
35 Word misinterpreted by Data in "The Schizoid Man" [TNG]
40 Black Cluster research vessel lost in "Hero Worship" [TNG]
41 Graves in "The Schizoid Man" [TNG]
42 Mind control expert in "Repression" [VGR]
44 Romero in "Journey's End" [TNG]
45 Gramilian ___ peas
47 New phrase for Data in "Where No One Has Gone Before" [TNG]
49 Leonard James ___, baby in "Friday's Child" [TOS]
51 Catch again
52 "___ of Fear" [TNG]
55 ___-jytsu, sport
59 Pig ___ poke
61 Phrase used by Data in *Insurrection*
66 Officer apparently killed in "Conspiracy" [TNG]
68 NFL legend Lou Groza's nickname
69 Sugar suffix
70 Top pilots
71 Actress Soto
72 Nothing
73 Edible seaweed
74 Gave a speech
75 Pipe turn

DOWN

1 Feudal slaves
2 Iona Maris role in "Workforce, Part I" [VGR]
3 Restrict a web search
4 Neelix's capacity
5 Film holder
6 Kazon-___ sect
7 Leveling wedge
8 List parts
9 Capt. Sisko's mother
10 Major golf tourney
11 He played Akorem Laan in "Accession" [DS9]
12 Word after induction or interface
13 "The Perfect ___" [TNG]
21 ___ *Dick* (19th-century Earth novel)
22 What Stella did to Harry Mudd
26 Gun a motor in neutral
28 Wanted poster letters
29 Cookie containers
30 Israeli airline
31 More cunning
33 Kind of tea enjoyed by V'Lar in "Fallen Hero" [ENT]
34 Confinement ___
35 Descendant of Jadzia Dax in "Children of Time" [DS9]
36 ___'Taral, Stephen Davies role in "Hippocratic Oath" [DS9]
37 Vidiian loved by the Doctor in "Lifesigns" [VGR]
38 George in "Cost of Living" [TNG]
39 Oil drilling structures
43 "___ walks in beauty ...": Byron
46 Daniel ___ Kim in "Blink of an Eye" [VGR]
48 "___ Life" [VGR]
50 Gi'___, Klingon who married a Romulan in "Birthright" [TNG]
53 Numbers game
54 Kaybok's bird-of-prey in "The Way of the Warrior" [DS9]
56 "To boldly go where ___ has gone before"
57 Langton who played the "Caretaker" [VGR]
58 Bringloidi leader Danilo in "Up the Long Ladder" [TNG]
59 Zeon prisoner in "Patterns of Force" [TOS]
60 Pleasant
62 Father of Jadzia Dax
63 Somewhat
64 Nicky the ___, holo-character in *First Contact*
65 "Barge of the ___" [VGR]
67 Gary Mitchell scored high in this ability

Raymond Hamel

ACROSS

1 Defender who dies in "Nemesis" [VGR]
6 Couples
10 Trader who captured Data in "The Most Toys" [TNG]
14 Kataan woman recalled by Picard in "The Inner Light" [TNG]
15 Starship access
16 Fibs
17 Where Quark was born
19 Fruity quaffs
20 Hammer end
21 Federation starship class
23 July hrs.
25 Mayweather and Ro
27 Odo once regenerated in one
28 Endings for employ
29 Asian goat
32 Skeptic's remark
34 Data's Spot, e.g.
35 Science Consultant on *The Motion Picture*
37 Magical word
38 Tot's three-wheeler
40 "Dark ___" [TNG]
41 Force ___
43 Cover
44 Comfy
45 J'naii leader in "The Outcast" [TNG]
46 Tutelary deity
47 Drug-busting org.
48 Archer befriends them in "Detained" [ENT]
51 Fools
52 "Weapon" made by The Doctor in "Macrocosm" [VGR]
55 Middle prefix
57 Enabran Tain's housekeeper
58 Ship destroyed in *The Search for Spock*
63 Soon
64 Vulcans don't do this
65 Bejal in "Rejoined" [DS9]
66 E Indian weights
67 Aleutian air base
68 General in "Sons and Daughters" [DS9]

DOWN

1 Ring official
2 Romulan brew drunk in *Nemesis*
3 Evergreen
4 Like Rom, at baseball
5 Rare goose
6 He plays Commander Tucker on *Enterprise*
7 *Kahs-___* (Vulcan coming-of-age ritual)
8 Saudi neighbors
9 Mistletoe piece
10 *U.S.S. Gorkon* and *I.K.S. Bortas*
11 Verdi opera
12 Scoff
13 Femur and fibula
18 "Amazing!"
22 "I don't step on ___, Major.": Odo ("Playing God")
23 Farm horse
24 Sound system
26 Where Rain worked in "Future's End" [VGR]
27 Chanteuse Edith
30 Spock's mother
31 Borg drones led by Lore
33 They recreated Rigel VII for Capt. Pike
34 Two per qt.
35 Teacher's-aide deg.
36 Probe that discovered Gomtuu in "Tin Man" [TNG]
39 Major Nerys' mother
42 Dermatiraelian plastiscine, for example
46 House finch
49 Dabo girl who married Rom
50 Saul's grandfather
51 "The Devil in the Dark" creature [TOS]
52 Latin-I word
53 *Voyager's* Seven of ___
54 Tiburon surveyor in "The Ship" [DS9]
56 Data's pet
59 Make a doily
60 Barros ___
61 Apnex ___ in "The Detector" [TNG]
62 Hospital areas: Abbr.

Sam Bellotto Jr.

ACROSS

1 *U.S.S. ___ Grande*
4 ___ Alpha V, Khan's planet
8 ___ Moss, Millennium Gate developer
14 Conclusion
15 *Generations* actor Ruck
16 Pregnant blight victim in "The Quickening" [DS9]
17 Comedienne Margaret
18 " ___ it my way..."
19 Precisely
20 Female astronomer in "Future's End" [VGR]
23 Pennsylvania city
24 Like Spock in *The Search for Spock*
28 ___ Leader Brone ("Nemesis" [VGR])
29 Raz in "The Last Outpost" [TNG]
31 Spanish gold
32 Midro player in "The Cloud Minders" [TOS]
35 Kids game
38 Captain's area
40 Felisa Howard's favorite flower in "Sub Rosa" [TNG]
43 "Dax" writer Peter Allen ___
47 Country with a flag like the Yangs
48 Actress Paquin
50 Capellan in "Friday's Child" [TOS]
51 It gets scanned
54 Greek dessert
57 He was Flavius in "Bread and Circuses" [TOS]
59 Slyer
62 Fishing line holder
63 1963 Martin Ritt film
64 Home of the cove palm in "Brothers" [TNG]
65 Karapleedeez in "We'll Always Have Paris" [TNG]
66 Prior to, to the Bard
67 ___ Woods on Bajor
68 Right away, to Dr. Crusher
69 Part of Chekov's old country

DOWN

1 Box up again
2 Spores were this in "This Side of Paradise" [TOS]
3 Nothing, to a Cardassian
4 Ship in "Chain of Command" [TNG]
5 Poet discussed in "Fair Haven" [VGR]
6 Romulan brainwashing La Forge in "The Mind's Eye" [TNG]
7 Epsilon ___ star system in *TOS*
8 Jettisons
9 Greg Ellis role in "What You Leave Behind" [DS9]
10 Bajoran merchant in "Rivals" [DS9]
11 "Obsession" [TOS] writer Wallace
12 What Vulcans never do, supposedly
13 Daniel ___ Kim in "Blink of an Eye" [VGR]
21 "I'm ___ a spy than you are": Garak
22 *The ___ Ending Sacrifice* (Cardassian novel)
25 "Mazel ___!"
26 Anger
27 ___ Caroli V, planet in "Allegiance" [TNG]
30 Indo-European
33 ___ Bato system in "The Most Toys" [TNG]
34 Planet in "The Maquis, Part II" [DS9]
36 French king
37 ___ III, shipyard site in "Defiant" [DS9]
39 Ate
40 Baby bear
41 Daniel ___ Henson in "Fortunate Son" [ENT]
42 W'___, father of Doran in "Sons and Daughters" [DS9]
44 Restraints for Porthos
45 Swallows
46 Defame
49 "To ___ friends...to family.": Picard toast
52 Paula in *The Motion Picture*
53 Jim in "Critical Care" [VGR]
55 Kirk vs. Gorn episode
56 Character in "Alliances" and "Maneuvers" [VGR]
58 Near-Earth asteroid
59 Corn on the ___
60 "Coming of ___" [TNG]
61 Astronaut Grissom

Raymond Hamel

ACROSS

1 Ark groupings
5 ___-pressed latinum
9 Identical
13 She plays Sato on *Enterprise*
14 Port Stanley's lake
15 Chief Medical Officer aboard *Enterprise* NX-01
16 Prologue follower
17 Catches a few z's
18 Sandwich-board words
19 Ancient doctor who "fathered" Data
22 Poet's preposition
23 Egyptian king
24 Prefix with badge
27 Inventor of warp drive in 2063
32 Quadrotriticale storage site
33 British bathroom
34 Klingon family units
35 Early *Star Trek* hairstyles
38 Caesar's 2005
40 Gag
41 Bridal wreath
43 German pronoun
45 Set a starship course (with "in")
46 Chief Medical Officer under Capt. Picard
50 Pitcher Emil
51 Where to register a TM
52 Highland turndown
53 Chief Medical Officer under Captain Kirk
59 "Spock's ___" [TOS]
62 Open a crack
63 Malcorian doctor in "First Contact" [TNG]
64 He won the Carrington Award in 2371 over Dr. Bashir
65 Star ___
66 Poet Khayyám
67 Revival cry
68 Fired
69 Electrical units

DOWN

1 Vulcan doctor murder suspect in "Suspicions" [TNG]
2 City on the Brazos
3 "___ take arms against...": Shak.
4 "___ Evil" [TNG]
5 Klingon warrior Martok's rank
6 North African port
7 Loose ones sink ships
8 Commander of the starship *U.S.S. Hood*
9 Chase flies
10 Computer key
11 Extinct New Zealand bird
12 Bus. phone
15 ___-Mul of the Lornak in "The Vengeance Factor" [TNG]
20 Comparative suffix
21 Response to a Regalian fleaspider bite
24 Flint built one on Holberg 917-G [TOS]
25 Kind of garage
26 Like a seine
27 Dashed
28 Salad plant
29 Beverly Crusher, to Wesley
30 Holodeck character created by Data to study humor
31 Kumquat's family
32 British guardsman's hat
36 Form of dilithium
37 ___ worms (*gagh* ingredient)
39 Camcorder part
42 Lowest female voice
44 Baby-changeling number sent out by the Founders [DS9]
47 Asteroid ship where McCoy married Natira
48 Capt. Kirk's older brother
49 Lt. Ilario who was killed in "Field of Fire" [DS9]
53 She portrayed Kes
54 Starship commanded by Picard's friend, Corey Zweller
55 Judge
56 Occurred
57 Communicator shape, circa 2364
58 Natasha and Ishara
59 Lingerie item
60 Quark's brother
61 "Coming of ___" [TNG]

Sam Bellotto Jr.

ACROSS

1 Sarandon in "Rivals" [DS9]
6 O'Henry's "The Gift of the ___"
10 "___ and Q" [TNG]
14 Tips to one side
15 Vulcan pin
16 Vigorous spirit
17 She played the Borg queen
19 Top-notch
20 Basketball official
21 In no time
22 Klingon drink
24 Volcano scaled by Kahless
26 "Mudd's Women" [TOS] director Harvey
27 Fire
28 Digging tool
31 Despot slain by Kahless
34 Yearn for
35 Trekkies, e.g.
37 Very many
38 Wedding site
39 Guiding ___, center of Talaxian afterlife
40 Master thrall in "The Gamesters of Triskelion" [TOS]
41 She played Roberta Lincoln in "Assignment: Earth" [TOS]
42 Chakotay's alias in "In The Flesh" [VGR]
43 Star system destroyed in "For The World Is Hollow..." [TOS]
45 Erica in "Infinite Regress" [VGR]
46 ___ phaser interlock
47 Quadrant in "Where Silence Has Lease" [TNG]
51 ___ III, planet attacked by Tom Riker in "Defiant" [DS9]
54 Amy Lindsay role in "Endgame, Part I" [VGR]
55 Galek ___, Cleponji captain in "Booby Trap" [TNG]
56 Kobayashi ___ scenario
57 Device used by Hoshi Sato
60 Leaf angle
61 Waikiki locale
62 ___ IV, dilithium-rich planet in "Pen Pals" [TNG]
63 Varis Sul portrayer Philips in "The Storyteller" [DS9]
64 ___ Penthe, Klingon penal planet
65 Indian wraps

DOWN

1 Josh in "Caretaker, Part I" [VGR]
2 Bajoran prisoner in "Indiscretion" [DS9]
3 Offspring of Tobin Dax
4 Company abbr.
5 John Durbin role in "Lonely Among Us" [TNG]
6 Romulan science officer in "The Next Phase" [TNG]
7 Tieran's physician in "Warlord" [VGR]
8 Jazz group's job
9 Cold drink
10 Klingon dish
11 He accused Dax of murder in "Dax" [DS9]
12 Inventor of the Tox Uthat in "Captain's Holiday" [TNG]
13 Party infiltrator in "Patterns of Force" [TOS]
18 Zen puzzle
23 "Obsession" [TOS] writer Wallace
25 He plays Capt. Jonathan Archer
26 Irritated Kelvan in "By Any Other Name" [TOS]
28 El-___ exchange, 3-D chess strategy
29 Grant of filmdom
30 Mayweather injured his in "Breaking the Ice" [ENT]
31 ___-lev carriage, vessel in "Rise" [VGR]
32 Actor Pooley in "Blink of an Eye" [VGR]
33 Holographic singer in "His Way" [DS9]
34 Dallas suburb
36 Tuvok's eldest son
38 Washing maching part
42 Sounds the clarions
44 ___ the Obscure in "Q-Less" [DS9]
45 Lunar mountain
47 Dr. Nel Apgar's widow [TNG]
48 Orphan Jeremy in "The Bonding" [TNG]
49 Samantha Wildman's daughter born on *Voyager*
50 Wall hanging
51 William Bastiani role in "Unification, Part II" [TNG]
52 Long skirt
53 Annika Hansen's mother
54 Bert who played a lion
58 *The Adventuress* novelist Santha Rama ___
59 Constellation known as 38 Across

Raymond Hamel

ACROSS

1 "Smart" guy
5 Voth Minister in "Distant Origin" [VGR]
10 Original Security Chief under Capt. Picard
13 Beach resort
14 Chow-yun creations in "The Die Is Cast" [DS9]
15 Turkish army leader
16 Traditional Vulcan dish
18 Sixty secs.
19 "A ___ Investigation" [DS9]
20 That girl
21 Type of Banean meat, often stewed
22 Electroplasma system ___
24 Emulate
26 Sgts.
28 Slanted fonts
30 Billingsley who portrays Dr. Phlox
31 Boss: Abbr.
32 Imagine
35 Hail, to Caesar
36 Bajoran hero freed by Kira Nerys
38 ___ tree (trapped)
39 Captain Garrett of the U.S.S. Enterprise-C
41 Word before storm or propulsion
42 Worf's souvenir from his first ritual hunt
43 ___ frequency
45 Governor of California in 2024
46 Suspended animation
47 Enterprise helmsman
49 Shakespeare title starter
50 ___-warp state
52 Spats
56 Turandot role
57 Klingon dish chosen by Riker in "A Matter of Honor" [TNG]
59 Inclined
60 Picard's Aunt ___ home remedies
61 South Pacific girl
62 Suffix for self
63 Dr. Noel
64 House add-ons

DOWN

1 Denubian ___
2 2002 Louisiana hurricane
3 Jacob's brother
4 Victim of Scalosians in "Wink of an Eye" [TOS]
5 Planet ruled by Orson
6 A small measure for Joseph Sisko
7 Giant creature in "The Immunity Syndrome" [TOS]
8 ___ pudding (dessert made by Neelix)
9 African cobra
10 Food item enjoyed only by Cardassians
11 Limber
12 Ensign or Captain
14 ___ Space Station K-7
17 Dohlman Elaan's native planet
21 Commander of the U.S.S. Drake killed at Minos
23 "Turbolift" is one
25 Shadow sites
26 Wesley's Squadron in "The First Duty" [TNG]
27 Klingon alcoholic beverage
29 Holodeck setting in "Emergence" [TNG]
30 Mason or Leyden
31 ___ juice (Ferengi drink)
33 Vulcan doctor in "Suspicions" [TNG]
34 Most Bajorans ornament one
36 Floral necklaces
37 Starship captains keep them
40 "Phage" [VGR] story author Timothy De ___
42 Voltaire or Onizuka
44 Haifa locale
45 Musical symbol
46 Gold-pressed latinum fractions
48 GI hangouts
49 Kirghizian range
51 Perry's creator
53 Comet feature
54 Like some Starfleet Academy exams
55 Noncoms
57 "I don't believe it!"
58 ___-Forward Lounge

Sam Bellotto Jr.

ACROSS

1 "You win!"
6 Battle of Klach ___ Brakt
10 Russian news agency
14 Like the Blight
15 Clothesline
16 Klingon spy in "Visionary" [DS9]
17 Skylit rooms
18 ___ Sky terrorist group in "The Chute" [VGR]
19 One of Icheb's old friends in "Child's Play" [VGR]
20 TNG episode in which Barclay develops a transporter phobia
23 Tongo ___ in "The Way to Eden" [TOS]
24 DS9 security head
25 She was Alexana in "The High Ground" [TNG]
27 Place side by side
31 Outpost ___-T-One in "Booby Trap" [TNG]
34 Worf, to Dax on DS9
35 Cardassian officer in "Necessary Evil" [DS9]
38 TNG episode in which Picard implements Transporter Code 14
42 Holographic world in "Shadowplay" [DS9]
43 Basilica center
44 Like a Klingon hit with a painstik
45 Emotion Tucker explains to Kov in "Fusion" [ENT]
47 Zorn was one in "Encounter at Fairpoint, Part I" [TNG]
50 Caithlin in The Final Frontier
51 Chicken ___ king
52 TOS episode in which a transporter splits Kirk in two
60 Harry Kim's friend in "Non Sequitur" [VGR]
62 Chancellor Durken in First Contact
63 Salinger in "Shakaar" [DS9]
64 Light tan
65 Romaine in "The Lights of Zetar" [TOS]
66 Cardassian star system in "Defiant" [DS9]
67 "And The Children Shall ___" [TOS]
68 Verve
69 Cybergeeks

DOWN

1 He played Mark in "Persistence of Vision" [VGR]
2 Low-cal
3 Jil in "Chain of Command, Part I" [TNG]
4 Bajoran solar-___ vessel
5 "Magnificent" figure in "Hero Worship" [TNG]
6 Smuggler Awa in "The Maquis, Part II" [DS9]
7 Engineering ensign in "Brothers" [TNG]
8 Sulu wielded one in "The Naked Time" [TOS]
9 Siberian river
10 Betazoid ___ Elbrun in "Tin Man" [TNG]
11 Maquis member in "Hunters" [VGR]
12 Vidiian scientist in "Faces" [VGR]
13 Holonovel character Bender in "Manhunt" [TNG]
21 "Falon's Journey" is one
22 Race encountered in "Renaissance Man" [VGR]
26 Cardassian novel The Never ___ Sacrifice
27 Alphabet openers
28 Austin ___ State U.
29 Echo ___ 607 in "The Arsenal of Freedom" [TNG]
30 Ran circles around
31 ___ Crabtree, first girlfriend of Tom Paris
32 Education level
33 Beta-___, The Doctor's family program in "Real Life"
35 Pesky insect
36 Jake Sakson role in "Counterpoint" [VGR]
37 Good review
39 Eagle's nest
40 "Badda-Bing Badda-Bang" [DS9] cowriter Behr
41 So far
45 How gagh is best served
46 Gamma ___, fallback position in "Redemption, Part II" [TNG]
47 "Journey to ___" [TOS]
48 Andrece in "I, Mudd" [TOS]
49 Suliban prisoner in "Detained" [ENT]
50 Poet Thomas
53 "By Any Other ___" [TOS]
54 "Skin of ___" [TNG]
55 Vedek ___ in "Rapture" [DS9]
56 "Magically" repaired item in "Spirit Folk" [VGR]
57 Saavik changes hers in The Wrath of Khan
58 Telepathic historian in "Violations" [TNG]
59 Capone battler
61 Misfiring firecracker

Raymond Hamel

ACROSS

1 Extra
6 *Enterprise* destroyed one in "Tomorrow Is Yesterday" [TOS]
9 Ferengi commander stranded in "Force of Nature" [TNG]
13 Slowly, in music
14 Sikarian who traded trajector technology to *Voyager*
16 "Sub ___" [TNG]
17 *Voyager* two-parter
19 Tobacco kiln
20 Immigrant's subj.
21 Trekkie, e.g.
22 Jawless fish
24 Prep a hypospray
26 Representative of the B'omar Sovereignty
27 *The Original Series* two-parter
32 Mine passage
35 UN agency
36 Archaeologist who discovered Ya'Seem
37 Tarchee ___
38 Where Captain Janeway grew up
41 Vardalos or Long
42 Had leftovers
44 Year in Spain
45 Beverages for Sulu and Picard
46 *Voyager* two-parter
50 Question opener
51 T'Pol never does this
55 *Star Trek: First ___* (1996)
58 Energy
59 Wood sorrel
60 Ambassador Lwaxana
61 *The Next Generation* two-parter
64 Fume
65 Ferengi arms dealer in "Unification" [TNG]
66 Peek-a-boo material
67 Alone, to an actress
68 Sato Hoshi's rnk.
69 Sharpened

DOWN

1 *Delta ___* shuttlecraft designed by Tom Paris
2 Security officer in "For the Cause" [DS9]
3 Totally
4 Missive: Abbr.
5 Tub sponge
6 Billingsley of Dr. Phlox fame
7 Sorbonne summer
8 Star system containing 31 Down
9 Bajoran spiritual entity
10 Emulate a mugato
11 African fox
12 Actress Jurado
15 Pack animal
18 Start of many a *Star Trek* scene
23 Atrea IV's was reliquefied in "Inheritance" [TNG]
25 Hubbell's roommate
26 Starship hijacked by Thomas Riker
28 Berlinghoff Rasmussen's century, in a way
29 *TNG* story editor Echevarria
30 Navigator killed by the *V'Ger* entity
31 See 8 Down
32 School for Starfleet trainees: Abbr.
33 Noonien Soong's creation
34 Roman road
38 Prefix for structure
39 "Fire" insect in "The Chute" [VGR]
40 Problem for some Betazoids
43 Jem'Hadar officer executed by Deyos
45 ___-ox compound given in "Rise" [VGR]
47 Opposed to verso
48 Prompt
49 Deanna Troi is one
52 Prytt Security Minister in "Attached" [TNG]
53 Sorbonne, for one
54 Made boards
55 Cores: Abbr.
56 Mountain: Comb. form
57 She accompanied Kirk to Tantalus V
58 Dowels
62 "The ___ Trap" [TOS]
63 Joey

Sam Bellotto Jr.

ACROSS

1 Holonovel character in "Heroes and Demons" [VGR]
6 Wandered
11 Ellen in "The Quality of Life" [TNG]
14 Bolshevism founder
15 Bajoran in "Accession" [DS9]
16 Mauna ___
17 "Honor ___ Thieves" [DS9]
18 Dr. Wykoff in "Shadows and Symbols" [DS9]
19 Deanna Troi's father
20 What "Charlie X" called Mr. Spock
22 Actress Karenina in "Haven" [TNG]
23 B'Etor's sister
24 Ves ___ in "Man of the People" [TNG]
25 ___-thorium device, weapon
28 ___ reference scan
29 Like Bendii syndrome
30 Lt. Nicoletti on *Voyager*
33 Prison satellite inmate in "The Chute" [VGR]
36 *TOS* episode that introduced Spock's nerve pinch
40 "By ___ Other Name" [TOS]
41 Ferengi emissary Par ___ in "The Perfect Mate" [TNG]
42 Kudak'___, Jem'Hadar warrior in "One Little Ship" [DS9]
43 Romulan beverage
44 Working as a volunteer
47 Bruce in "Blood Fever" [VGR]
50 Jill in "The Abandoned" [DS9]
52 Like Spock's homeworld
53 Instrument played by Spock
58 ___ *transit gloria mundi*
59 Jal ___, first maje of the Kazon-Ogla
60 *Mauk-*___, Klingon ritual
61 Half a humanoid in "Macrocosm" [VGR]
62 Meribor's mother in "The Inner Light" [TNG]
63 Cluster in "The Vengeance Factor" [TNG]
64 Double curve
65 Dutch painter Jan
66 ___ VI, planet in "Time Squared" [TNG]

DOWN

1 Ruse
2 Ancient people of Gaul
3 Grandson of Eve
4 He was killed by Liam Bilby in 17 Across
5 Ensign Martine in "Balance of Terror" [TOS]
6 *U.S.S. Voyager* crew member
7 Sector visited by *Enterprise* in "Future Imperfect" [TNG]
8 ___ II, deserted planet in "Skin of Evil" [TNG]
9 Work units
10 Valerian ship *Sherval* ___ in "Dramatis Personae" [DS9]
11 "___ of an Eye" [VGR]
12 Bajoran shopkeeper in "Rivals" [DS9]
13 Ruler's daughter in "The Outrageous Okona" [TNG]
21 ___ the Obscure in "Q-Less" [DS9]
22 Chicken ___ Sisko
24 Marsha Hunt role in "Too Short a Season" [TNG]
25 James in "The Godfather"
26 Rowdy party
27 Canine command
28 "___ HIHoH" (Klingon for "now" or "today")
29 Vitamin spec.
31 *Enterprise*, in "Tomorrow is Yesterday" [TOS]
32 Mr. Homn portrayer
33 Tubular pasta
34 Ullian delegation member in "Violations" [TNG]
35 System of transmission conduits: Abbr.
37 Alexander in "Nor the Battle to the Strong" [DS9]
38 *Sha Ka* ___, Vulcan heaven
39 ___ 3, Eminiar VII official in "A Taste of Armageddon" [TOS]
43 "Trials ___ Tribble-ations" [DS9]
45 FDR's "Blue Eagle"
46 Klingon prison Rura ___
47 Sew loosely
48 Cardassian star system in "Defiant" [DS9]
49 Marva in "Persistence of Vision" [VGR]
50 Plakson who played a Q in "The Q and the Grey" [VGR]
51 Straighten
53 Former enemy of Krios ("The Perfect Mate" [TNG])
54 Mugato feature in "A Private Little War" [TOS]
55 Shakespeare's river
56 Italia capital
57 Silaran in "The Darkness and the Light" [DS9]
59 Legal matter

Raymond Hamel

ACROSS

1 ___-ovo-vegetarian
6 Tuvok's wife
10 Romulan who contacted *Voyager* through a micro-wormhole
14 Tantamount
15 Louvre hangings
16 Ending for Louis
17 Spock faked this in "The Enterprise Incident" [TOS]
20 Night blessing of ___-El
21 Worf portrayer
22 Sicilian spouter
23 A vote "for"
25 Under the weather
26 It hides Romulan birds-of-prey
34 Ferengi Liquidator
35 Start a tongo game
36 Performed
37 Large Ferengi feature
38 Bonne who was Ruth in "Shore Leave" [TOS]
41 "The Deadly Years" subject [TOS]
42 Sigmoid curve
43 Companion of Ares
44 Bajoran national executed by Odo
46 Klingon hand weapon
50 Vulcans don't do this
51 Green shade
52 Trader who frequented the Nekrit Supply Depot
55 Aleutian air base
58 Riker is fond of this planet
62 Federation starship weapons
65 Aurelan, to David Marcus
66 Lane divider
67 Peter in "School Ties"
68 Not we
69 City on the Irtysh
70 Space sector in "The Muse" [DS9]

DOWN

1 Tax
2 Word form for "water"
3 ___-de-sac (alleys)
4 Faster-than-light particle
5 Schnozz add-on
6 Furor
7 Anchorage
8 *Joie de vivre*
9 Normandy ship
10 Planet in "Journey to Babel" [TOS]
11 Market
12 "Come ___!"
13 Island SSE of Tahiti
18 Fargo loc.
19 Goro portrayer in "The Paradise Syndrome" [TOS]
24 Frequents Sisko's Creole Kitchen
25 Unemployed
26 It's investigated in "Oasis" [ENT]
27 Elder of Duras' two sisters
28 Cluster in "Too Short a Season" [TNG]
29 Commanding officer Kira
30 ___-class Cardassian warship
31 Wyoming neighbor
32 Kira smokes one in "Our Man Bashir" [DS9]
33 "The Way to ___" [TOS]
34 Communicator signal
39 Lamarr in *My Favorite Spy*
40 Cry of alarm
45 Leonard Nimoy achieved this as Spock
47 Kirk's Chief Engineer
48 Protocol Master for Minister Campio
49 "___ and away!"
52 Young oyster
53 Nope
54 Style
55 Source of 4 Down
56 A lot
57 Kirk's voyage
59 New Rochelle campus
60 Bajoran word for "swamp"
61 Italian wine city
63 Sgt. or Cpl.
64 Academia URL suffix

Sam Bellotto Jr.

ACROSS

1 *Star Trek II: The ___ of Khan*
6 ___ shuttlebay
10 Supply ship in "A Fistful of Datas" [TNG]
14 Kazon-___
15 Jonathan Del ___, Hugh in "I, Borg" [TNG]
16 ___ II, destination in "The Offspring" [TNG]
17 Fix
18 Human, to Nomad in "The Changeling" [TOS]
19 ___ Danar in "The Hunted" [TNG]
20 *Warped Factors* author
23 Hit the slopes
24 Like the superlative rose
28 Buddy
31 Father of "gangsta" rap
34 Christi Henshaw player in "Booby Trap" [TNG]
35 ___ *ulat*, joining ceremony phrase in "Favorite Son" [VGR]
37 Butterine
39 Creative Writing instructor at Starfleet Academy
40 He directed "Hippocratic Oath" [DS9]
43 Lines up
44 Italian volcano
45 Building wings
46 Food found in "Starship Down" [DS9]
48 "The Lights of Zetar" [TOS] director Kenwith
50 Markoffian ___ lizard
51 Andorian fetaure
53 ___-birds of Regulus V
55 He directed *The Search for Spock*
61 ___ Marie Hupp in "Galaxy's Child" [TOS]
64 *Kobayashi ___*
65 C African republic
66 Kudak'___, Jem'Hadar in "One Little Ship" [DS9]
67 Kelbonite and magnesite
68 The O'Briens' babysitter on DS9
69 Presidential option
70 Meribor player in "The Inner Light" [TNG]
71 Radioactive element

DOWN

1 "That was close!"
2 Eternal City
3 Son of Adam
4 Colors
5 Cardassian starship class
6 ___-to'Vor, Klingon ritual
7 River in "Concerning Flight" [VGR]
8 More frigid
9 Used
10 Cybernetic being
11 John Kim player in "Author, Author" [VGR]
12 Bajoran magistrate Faren in "The Storyteller" [DS9]
13 Mouths
21 Underwater filming expert Browning
22 Boise's state
25 Matriculates
26 Like Kirk in "The Deadly Years" [TOS]
27 96-year-old Drayan in "Innocence" [VGR]
28 Seska player Hackett
29 Son of the Ilari Autoarch in "Warlord" [VGR]
30 Stuntman Yakima
32 Dresden's river
33 Uneven Ferengi features
36 He played Kalo in "A Piece of the Action" [TOS]
38 French river
41 United
42 Ventaxian leader in "Devil's Due" [TNG]
47 Sundial part
49 Class-M world in "A Matter of Honor" [TNG]
52 Apprentice engineer in "The Forsaken" [DS9]
54 Ezral's daughter in "Oasis" [ENT]
56 ___ *IV module* in "One Small Step" [VGR]
57 *VGR* and *ENT* director of photography Marvin V. ___
58 "Frame of ___" [TNG]
59 Word form of "mountain"
60 Obsidian Order agent in "Second Skin" [DS9]
61 Ullian historian in "Violations" [TNG]
62 Tried foraiga
63 "King" Cole or Segaloff

Raymond Hamel

ACROSS

1 "Ugly ___ of mostly water" (humans, to Velarians) [TNG]
5 Flagpole
9 Kind of rations on *Enterprise-D*
12 Uncle of Kes
14 Fatty
16 Arctic explorer
17 Ferengi Rule of Acquisition #217 (with 26-A)
19 Suffix with corbom?
20 Prefix with nagus or hadar
21 Betty Ford Clinic, e.g.
22 Energy weapon in "The Cage"
24 "Even ___ speak ..."
25 Sam or Aurelan
26 See 17 Across
32 Mirich in "Relics" [TNG]
33 U.S. narcotics agcy.
34 Ensign Peter on *Enterprise-D*
36 Kind of bread
37 Vulcan gunrunner and Maquis member
41 Daughter of Cadmus
42 Florence-Venice dir.
43 Zet's friend in "Renaissance Man" [VGR]
44 *U.S.S. Rutledge* officer duplicated by Cardassians
46 Ferengi Rule of Acquisition #10
51 George De La ___ in "The Arsenal of Freedom" [TNG]
52 "___ Fall in Love"
53 Throbbed
55 Slope
57 Bradley and Begley
60 Kiwi kin
61 Ferengi Rule of Acquisition #95
64 Personals
65 "Splish Splash" singer
66 Double star in Orion
67 Arikara
68 Planetary system in "A Time to Stand" [DS9]
69 ___ Stromgren (planet)

DOWN

1 Turkish bigwigs
2 Baseball brothers
3 Ferengi delicacy
4 With par, it's a long way
5 Beverly Crusher, to Wesley
6 Class-M planet in "The Enemy Within"
7 Southern Slav
8 Deuce, for example
9 Planet where slaves were kept for gaming
10 Mulgrew on *Voyager*
11 Sly Ferengi look
13 Rakonian swamp-rat milieus
15 Lovsky in "Amok Time"
18 Canadian prov.
23 Tate hangings
24 Thus, in Toledo
25 Calloway's love in "Eye of the Beholder" [TNG]
26 Captain Braxton's timeship
27 Takarian monetary unit
28 ___ generator (cloaking technology)
29 T'Pol has a problem with them
30 "Little Green ___" [DS9]
31 Taresian woman who pursued Harry Kim
35 She accompanied Kirk to Tantalus V
38 "All I ask is a tall ship ___ load of contraband...": Quark
39 Bajoran religious leader
40 Partner in crime
45 Project followers
47 Brogue width
48 Terminated
49 Chief Engineer B'___ Torres
50 Point in one direction
53 Klingon battle cruiser
54 "___ of Honor" [TNG]
55 Facile
56 Burrow
57 "The City on the ___ of Forever" [TOS]
58 Battle the bulge
59 Tasha Yar's daughter
62 Amerind totem pole
63 Needle

Sam Bellotto Jr.

ACROSS

1 Steinberg in "First Contact" [TNG]
5 Delta ___ IV star system in "The Survivors" [TNG]
9 What the Hirogen do
14 Singer Timi
15 Shrinking sea
16 Star system in "Heart of Glory" [TNG]
17 ___ Garak
18 "That Which Survives" [TOS] director Wallerstein
19 Touch-___ downwarping
20 James T. Kirk quote: Part 1 ("The Galileo Seven" [TOS])
23 Brain scan
24 Actress Loseth in "Life Support" [DS9]
25 Baby's skin condition
27 *Toh'Kaht* first officer in "Dramatis Personae" [DS9]
31 "Wolf in ___ Fold" [TOS]
32 Attorney Shaw in "Court Martial" [TOS]
33 James T. Kirk quote: Part 2
39 Jim Shimoda portrayer in "The Naked Now" [TNG]
40 Jury members
41 Ancient Roman coin
42 James T. Kirk quote: Part 3
45 Toy train standard
47 Billy Burke role in "Second Skin" [DS9]
48 Briam player in "The Perfect Mate" [TNG]
50 Dance done by Spock in "Plato's Stepchildren" [TOS]
55 London lavatory
56 Ship's record
57 James T. Kirk quote: Part 4
62 "Menage ___" [TNG]
64 Mideast Terran land
65 Cherub, at Notre Dame
66 *Enterprise* rear area
67 *Voyager* episode where Sklar dies
68 French city between the Rhône and Saône rivers
69 Captain in "Fortunate Son" [ENT]
70 Old ___ in "Catspaw" [TOS]
71 Supervisor in "Gravity" [VGR]

DOWN

1 Looked over
2 ___ of Acquisition
3 Bahr in "Endgame" [VGR]
4 Vie
5 Showily enthusiastic
6 Region
7 *U.S.S. Ajax* captain in "Tapestry" [TNG]
8 Juggler Selznick in "Cost of Living" [TNG]
9 Fleet admiral in "Redemption, Part 1" [TNG]
10 ___ Ru, mystery probe in "The Changeling" [TOS]
11 Mythical planet in "When the Bough Breaks" [TNG]
12 "Inter Arma Enim Silent ___" [DS9]
13 *U.S.S. Odyssey* captain in "The Jem'Hadar" [DS9]
21 "Skin of ___" [TNG]
22 Swearing-in statements
26 Lt. Barclay's nickname
27 He played Goro in "The Paradise Syndrome" [TOS]
28 Romulan-Borg in "Unity" [VGR]
29 *Nautilus* captain
30 Kes player Jennifer
34 Nimian ___ salt
35 Singer Guthrie
36 Beatrice in "Persistence of Vision" [VGR]
37 Toy building block
38 River through Flanders
40 Vulcan ear feature
43 Elbrun in "Tin Man" [TNG]
44 ___ Syndrome in "Violations" [TNG]
45 Blooper
46 Cascade ___
49 Mariposa Colony members in "Up the Long Ladder" [TNG]
50 Dr. Philip Boyce carried one
51 Actress Lenya
52 Concur
53 Capt. Jellico's ship in "Chain of Command, Part I" [TNG]
54 John Prosky role in "Friendship One" [VGR]
58 Smooth sailing
59 Jaresh-___, Federation President
60 Start of the Klingon divorce declaration
61 "Phage" [VGR] cowriter Skye
63 ___ Lote, engineering expert in "True-Q" [TNG]

Raymond Hamel

ACROSS

1 "Death ___" [VGR]
5 Ramsey's ship that hit an asteroid ("Angel One" [TNG])
9 Young herring
14 1975 Wimbledon winner
15 "Sub ___" [TNG]
16 He was Amaros in "The Maquis, Part I" [DS9]
17 Brother of Kira Nerys
18 Ferengi DaiMon in "the Price" [TNG]
19 Cardassian teen in "The Dogs of War" [DS9]
20 Alture VII relaxation ___ ("Birthright, Part I" [TNG])
22 Stubborn
24 Deanna Troi's father
25 Sugar suffix
26 Jibalian seven-spice omelette ingredient
30 Cardassian Quark bribed in "The Wire" [DS9]
34 Wound
35 Ru'afo in *Insurrection*
37 Ledosian flying instructor in "Natural Law" [VGR]
38 Enzyme suffix
39 "Future's ___" [VGR]
40 Security field subsystem ___
41 Ba'ku enemy in *Insurrection*
43 Pennants
45 "For the World Is Hollow ___ Have Touched the Sky" [TOS]
46 What Layna said Torres was in "Muse" [VGR]
48 Goth, for one ("Rise" [VGR])
50 Bern river
51 Curve
52 "Second ___" [TNG]
56 Space station in *The Motion Picture*
60 Annette who was Karina in "Visionary" [DS9]
61 Female Klingon mating call
63 German article
64 Jumja seller on Deep Space 9's Promenade
65 Neonate
66 She was Lola in "His Way" [DS9]
67 Tinnitus problem
68 ___ II, starbase destination in "The Offspring" [TNG]
69 "The Man ___" [TOS]

DOWN

1 Faster-than-light speed
2 Elbe tributary
3 "Scat!"
4 Redjac's victim in "Wolf in the Fold" [TOS]
5 "Baroner" was Kirk's alias on this planet
6 Fortress of ___ in "Bride of Chaotica" [VGR]
7 *Mir* successor
8 *Endeavour's* org.
9 ___ down (land in water)
10 Vulcan soup
11 Delta ___ IV in "The Survivers" [TNG]
12 Eminiar leader in "A Taste of Armageddon" [TOS]
13 Like Terran lemons
21 Super Bowl shout
23 Portal
26 Kind of pistol in "Broken Bow" [ENT]
27 Damar kills him in "Tacking Into The Wind" [DS9]
28 Tsu in "Favorite Son" [VGR]
29 *Voyager* crewmember in "Learning Curve" [VGR]
30 Kirk's "com" communicator
31 "Young child" in "Innocence" [VGR]
32 Home world of Dalen Quaice ("Remember Me" [TNG])
33 "Time and ___" [VGR]
36 The Doctor's restorative for Torres ("Faces" [VGR])
42 Vanessa Williams' *Deep Space Nine* role
43 Food and drink
44 Robin in "Mortal Coil" [VGR]
45 ___ Philosophies, Starfleet Academy course
47 Caretaker or Suspiria, e.g. ("Cold Fire" [VGR])
49 Ovid's "___ Amatoria"
52 Biggers sleuth
53 "___ Worship" [TNG]
54 "___ ask is a tall ship and a star...": Masefield
55 Jarvis' wife in "Wolf in the Fold" [TOS]
56 Penal colony site in "Whom Gods Destroy" [TOS]
57 Neelix called Paris this in "Parturition" [VGR]
58 Karapleedeez in "Conspiracy" [TNG]
59 Half-moon tide
62 Patronize the Celestial Cafe

John M. Samson

ACROSS

1 Prof's helpers: Abbr.
4 "Honor ___ Thieves" [DS9]
9 Vidiian feature
13 Cell energizer
14 Burton who plays La Forge
15 City ENE of Essen
16 *Enterprise* Season One cliffhanger
18 Third host to the Dax symbiont
19 Vulcan beverages
20 Where Uhura was born
22 Andorian blue feature
23 Prefix for path
25 Dixon Hill holodeck program thug
27 "The Enemy ___" [TOS]
32 Orange skin
35 Itinerary data
37 "___ Leave" [TOS]
38 Film where Riker marries Troi
41 Lake in Sweden
42 Letek's superior in "The Last Outpost" [TNG]
43 Reason for a trip to Risa
44 Romulus or Remus
46 Starship class
48 Peter in *M*
50 "Skin of ___" [TNG]
53 *Excelsior* commander Sulu
56 Made level
58 Drayan encountered by Tuvok in "Innocence" [VGR]
59 *Enterprise* series premier
62 Sentient
63 Par in "The Perfect Mate" [TNG]
64 Outlaw in "A Fistful of Datas" [TNG]
65 Tsunkatse death match organizer
66 Salli ___ Richardson in "Second Sight" [DS9]
67 Valerian vessel *Sherval* ___

DOWN

1 Australian island: Abbr.
2 Location of secret Maquis launch site
3 Amanda Grayson's son
4 Methane or ethane, e.g.
5 Talks like Spot
6 Macrogametes
7 Abbr. on a runabout console
8 ___ Plume of Agosoria [ENT]
9 Conscious start
10 Trellan reptile, for short
11 Terellian cargo freighter crash survivor in 2363
12 Marina Del ___
15 What the Karagite Order is for
17 "___ of Time" [DS9]
21 Handful
23 Fabrina's planetary group, e.g.
24 Leader of Kira's resistance cell
26 Always, to Donne
28 Ship belonging to Seven of Nine's parents
29 Doublet tights
30 Rainbow goddess
31 Gravity well, to a singularity alien
32 Invitation letters
33 Typeface abbr.
34 Visitor who plays a Bajoran
36 "Trip" Tucker has a distaste for this meat
39 "The Squire of Gothos" [TOS]
40 Epsilon ___ (S Hemisphere star)
45 *Fal-___-pan* (Vulcan rite)
47 Scout vessel in *The Motion Picture*
49 100 kopecks
51 Laid up
52 ___ root stew
53 Bunker Hill general
54 Persia now
55 "It was fun ... oh my" are his last words
56 Planet at war with Zeon
57 Highway felons
58 Polar ice ___
60 USG's Gray counterpart
61 20th-century U.S. Navy spy org.

Sam Bellotto Jr.

01

```
H A R A   O R U M   E R M A
S T O R E   B O N E   V A A L
H O O K S P I D E R   E Z R I
  A K A A R   E A R N   O L A
    R I O T   S I E R R A
A N S I   F R A Y   C A B
T A L A R I A N   T H E T A
U Z I   E T Y S H R A   A R R
L I M E D   H E A R T S O F
  E D O   L A A N   O T I S
  I D A N I A   T S A R
A L E   E N S E   O R I O N
L A V A   L U N G M A G G O T
B R I G   E M I T   B A L O K
S I L O   T A M S   N A N O
```

02

```
U P T O N   F A L A   B A E R
R O U T E   T P E L   O M N I
S U T H E R L A N D   T A D S
A R S E N E   R D A   A R A K
    R A C H T   R E N O R A
C O S   H A Y   D A L Y
O V E R   P E N K   I B O R G
B A R I S   N E T   M A R I L
B L O O P   A L A S   Y E T O
    G O S S   H T A   L A B
O B E R T H   A G A T E
Z I N A   O R R   D O R A D O
A K I N   W E L L I N G T O N
B E N D   E M I T   C O R I N
A L A E   R I N D   E T A N A
```

03

```
R I C H   W A F T   M A N
A B R O M   I N R O   G A L E
R A Y W A L S T O N   A R I D
E R O   R A H   N O T I C E S
    D I R E C T   A L A N
S H A U N   S E I S M A L
T E L F A S   N E L S   A P T
A R I F   N I T R O   E I R E
T A C   C A N A   B E R M A N
  E L O G I U M   L I O N S
  S K I N   T R O M A C
F E R E N G I   K A I   T A L
O R I G   M A D L Y N R H U E
A U G E   A T N O   E A R T H
M M E   N E A R   P O O R
```

04

```
W O R F   R O S S   R O B I N
A N O A   E V I L   U R A N O
T E A R   D I N A   S E T T I
T I M R U S S   V I S I T O R
    E N T   L I L
W I L L I A M   B L A L O C K
O R E L   R E M U S   Y U L E
O I E   K E S   N E A
D S T S   S O R E N   S C A T
S H A T N E R   D A N C E R S
    E E E   T A I
F L O W E R S   J A N E W A Y
R E G A L   T O E S   N O D E
I D A R E   A D A H   C O A T
N A T T Y   N O N A   E L M O
```

05

```
D A T A . B A S E . . P A D
A L I C E . E D A M . L E N O
B E T H D E L T A I . U N T O
O S O . G A I . T R A C T O R
. . T E R E S A . R I A S .
A K A A R . F O R E V E R
B A R A S H . L A L A . U F O
I N C R . I D I N I . A S A P
E T H . S E R A . M A R I N A
. A C T R E S S . L E I G H
. A N Y A . A V E S T A .
G R I S S O M . C I A . B L T
R E S T . C E L T R I S I I I
A N I S . T R I O . R I K E R
M A V . . O S A R . G E N E
```

06

```
S T R U T . P I P E R . D U M
T E E R O . A D I E U . R N A
A S S I M I L A T E D . V I C
N T H . A R I . . O R A T E
. . C L A S S M P L A N E T
A L C O A . C O I F E D .
N A H S K . D O N T . O A F
B R A T . P E R K Y . A R V A
O D N . L A P S . O N E I L
. C A R O L I . P A N D A
T H E W A Y T O E D E N .
R E L A Y . . R O N . P E R
E L L . M E L V I N B E L L I
E D O . E S A A K . A R I A S
D E R . R A Y N A . R E E S E
```

07

```
A K I R A . J E F F S . T E R
L I N E S . A L I L Y . E L I
T R A C T O R B E A M . C A D
. A T L E C . E L M . H A G
. A R A S . D E F E N S E
L A R I . M O O S . R O O
E L E M S P U R . B O S L I C
O O P . C A P T A I N . O S U
V U L C A N . H R O T H G A R
. I A L . T O T S . E Y R E
N U C L E A R . S H A K .
A H A . R I G . I S A A C
G U T . T R A N S P O R T E R
U R O . N A L A S . N A T T O
S A R . G U S T S . E S A A K
```

08

```
B A N K . H O M E . D A L E D
E P E E . A G U E . A W A R E
A S T A . N U L L . K E S L A
D E S T R O Y . S M A S H E R
. . I O N . . I L O .
L T O N E I L . O C A M P A N
O M A G . V A G R A . E I R E
V E S . . R O D . . P E R
A N I J . O G D E N . B E N Y
L I S E T T E . K A T E R A S
. . L E T . . P A N .
E M O L S O N . K I M B A L L
G A L I S . V A R N . E Z I O
G R A C E . E R I N . C A M P
S Y N O N . K A T E . K N E E
```

09

```
V O I D . P R A K . H U S K
O N N A . H O R N . P A S T A
Y E T I . I T O O . E L A A N
. R O M U L A N W A R B I R D
. . O I L . N O G . D E A
S C A N T I E R . K I N .
U H D . P O U T . U T H A T
B A J O R A N W O R M H O L E
S I S K O . S O N A . S T A
. E L I . N O N F A T A L
T W A . L T S . C C L
H U M P B A C K W H A L E S
U H U R A . A I R E . O R T A
L A S E R . B R E R . U N U M
E N E S . S A N S . R E N E
```

10

```
M O M S . K O A L A . T I N Y
A Z A N . H U R O N . O N E A
G A R O . I C I N G . M A W R
D A Y O F T H E D O V E .
A L L P R O . S O L O I S T S
. . U M A . N A N . A R T
O U T F I E L D . . S H O O
S P E C T R E O F T H E G U N
A S E A . . A T R O C I T Y
G E T . M T V . L A B .
E T H E R E A L . M I T E N A
. . M I R R O R M I R R O R
M I R I . R A R E E . O M R I
I G E L . O N E I L . S A V E
R O G A . R I N D S . E T A L
```

11

```
N A T ■ N A V A L ■ T W E E T
E R A ■ O F A G E ■ R H A D A
X E P O L I T E S ■ A E R I E
U N I S E X ■ D E F I A N T ■
S A R I N ■ ■ ■ E N T ■ ■ ■
■ ■ E N C ■ G O R ■ O C T O
I L A R I O ■ R O E ■ N O E L
C Y R ■ S U Z A N N E ■ L T D
K L A V ■ N I N ■ G N O M E S
Y E T O ■ C O D ■ I N A ■ ■
■ ■ X V I ■ ■ ■ A S S O C
■ E P S I L O N ■ A N I M A L
C L E O N ■ H O S H I S A T O
A I S L E ■ O R A M A ■ R E N
B E T A S ■ H A G E N ■ T R E
```

12

```
K A R R ■ H A R U ■ B A N E S
I L I A ■ E L I S ■ A D E L E
P A L M ■ A I L S ■ A R U B A
P R E S E R V E R S ■ O T A R
■ ■ ■ C A S E Y ■ H A I R ■
E S C O R T ■ M A N T O O S
S T O O P ■ A K A R Y ■ N H L
A A R P ■ H R O M I ■ C I A O
A N D ■ D E E L A ■ L A U R A
K O R I N A S ■ F A T M A N
■ ■ A M A L ■ K I O W A ■ ■
N E Z U ■ Y E O M A N R O S S
E D I T H ■ G R A M ■ I T H E
R E N T E ■ G A G E ■ N E A L
O N E A M ■ S L E D ■ A L G A
```

13

```
E S O Q Q ■ K H A N ■ H I K E
N E H R U ■ E M M A ■ O V I D
T E R S A ■ T O E S ■ L O R E
O D E ■ D E R ■ B A J O R A N
■ ■ R I A ■ A L E G ■ ■ ■
N A E ■ A R C O S ■ D R I E R
E N G I N E E R ■ A N N A ■
E V E N T ■ L B S ■ K M P E C
L I S T ■ ■ I P R E S U M E
A L T E R ■ S T A I N ■ T Y S
■ ■ R O T O ■ C O T ■ ■ ■
U N I F O R M ■ E T A ■ B A T
P A R A ■ O R U M ■ N A O M I
O T I C ■ I A N A ■ N O M A D
N O S E ■ S W A N ■ A K A R Y
```

14

```
U R G E ■ E L A S ■ H A D T O
S E A L ■ T A C O ■ A R R O W
E T R E ■ A N I J ■ N O M A N
R I V E R S I D E I O W A ■ ■
I R I N A ■ ■ F T L ■ R Y E
D E N ■ D E L B ■ S I F T E R
■ ■ G I G O L O ■ L I S A
■ B L O O M I N G T O N ■ ■
C H A O ■ E S C R O W ■ ■ ■
F O R B E S ■ S E E M ■ M S G
L E T ■ M H O ■ ■ A K A A R
■ L A B A R R E F R A N C E
O P E R A ■ N A R A ■ F A R E
A S T E R ■ A V I S ■ A D E N
S I T A K ■ K E N T ■ R A D S
```

15

```
A T O Z ■ S K L A R ■ A T O A
L U T E ■ T E A C H ■ B A N S
O R N E ■ A L P H A W A V E S
N E E ■ R L S ■ D O R I A N
G I R A F F E ■ M A R C ■ ■
■ ■ C O L Y U S ■ F A C T O
S T A T U E ■ L E T ■ R O D
B E T A R E N N E R C L O U D
E R R ■ T O A ■ E R U P T S
S P I C Y ■ R E P A I R ■ ■
■ ■ R U J I ■ E S T E B A N
A V I A T E ■ S T U ■ R O E
D E L T A F L Y E R ■ F A R R
A T I E ■ F I B R E ■ C I T Y
H O A R ■ S T O S S ■ A N A S
```

16

```
S L O W ■ R A Y S ■ M U D D S
H O L O ■ A B E E ■ I N E R T
A C E R ■ N I N E ■ S I A N A
W H O M G O D S D E S T R O Y
■ ■ H A R E ■ ■ D I E ■ ■
L T B O M A ■ A R G O S I A N
A Y A L A ■ C L E A N ■ D R O
C L U E ■ S O L A R ■ L I E S
E E E ■ E E L E R ■ S T O N E
D R R A M S E Y ■ D E M M A S
■ ■ D I K ■ C O M A ■ ■
O R B I T A L H A B I T A T S
R O O S T ■ I O N A ■ S U R E
A D E L E ■ A M A R ■ O T E L
L E N O R ■ M O R A ■ N O E L
```

17

```
A S A . . S L I D . . T A M E
M A S . A D E L E . C A D E T
O T T . M L E I G H H U D E C
K O R O B . K A R Y A . N T H
. . O R E K . . E M M Y . . .
G E N E R O D D E N B E R R Y
E D O . . H E R . . E N E R O
N I M . A L W A N I R . C A D
I T E A R . . I N N . . A T E
C H R I S T I N E C H A P E L
. . . R E P S . . H E A T . .
A T F . N A L A S . L A U R A
L W A X A N A T R O I . R O M
M A J E L . N O T A X . E S A
A S O N . . D E A R . . D A R
```

18

```
U S S R . K I L E Y . P A G H
N A P E . I R I N A . O R R A
F R A T . R A N O R . L E A N
E D I T H K E E L E R . E N D
D A N I E L . . A T O L L . .
. . . K R A F T . H O U S K A
A T M . N E A P . D S H O N
R A I N . D E N E B . H A N A
A B R O M . S A R I . . W O N
L U A R A N . S U N A D . . .
. . . M I R E S . O L I A N A
A N A . C A R O L M A R C U S
M O N A . T O M E I . G O R P
A V E L . E K I N A . E S S E
R A E L . N A T A L . S T E N
```

19

```
M O R P H . O K O N A . T A T
U T E R O . B I P E D . O D E
M I N O R . S L U G O C O L A
. C A P T A I N S . S O L A R
. . H A N D . . . I S I S . .
A N N E . D I R . S Y N . . .
M O O T . R A E . K A S I D Y
O N O . P O N F A R R . N A E
K O R A I I . I R R . M A T A
. . L E D . T I E . A D A R
R E M I . . . A E O N . . .
O N I C E . J O N A T H A N
G R E E N H O R N . O U T E R
E O N . V E N T U . E N N A N
R L S . Y A N A S . S T O P S
```

20

```
L O R I . H A R T E . T H O T
I C O N . U H U R A . E A R L
N E S T . P O L O S . D A R O
K A S I D Y Y A T E S . K A R
E N A M O R . . H I P P O .
. . E L I A S . N O O N A N
N O W . T A R A L . T H I N E
G R I P . N O R E P . L A A N
O T N E R . N A K E D . N N E
S A N R I C . S A R E K . . .
. . A E S O P . S E R I A L
J U D . A L L A S O M O R P H
A L A I . T A L O N . N A R A
N I M S . A T A R A . O T I S
A S I S . R E N E E . S E L A
```

21

```
S P O C K . P R I N . H E A L
T I G R E . H E L L . U C L A
O N L Y A F O O L F I G H T S
A T A B . A T S . N O O S E
. . A F R O . M A C R . .
I N A B U R N I N G H O U S E
N E R Y S . L O U . L O W
C U E . E S C A P E S . A R I
A R T . O R R . C O N A N
N O E N E M Y I S B O R I N G
. . I L E O . I O W A . .
S P A C E . E L M . N E T S
H E D O E S N T E A T G A G H
A R I L . D O R N . K E S H A
P I N E . I G E T . O S T A R
```

22

```
H U G H . S T E W . A C I D S
A T O A . A R V A . L O V A L
R A N T . R E A R . E N A R A
T H E C A G E . M A N T R A P
. . H R E . . D I E . .
A L D E A N S . M A S S E T T
T O E R . T A M A R . T R A Y
T U B . . N A R . . R U K
I S I K . S T R I P . B O R E
C Y N T H I A . L A P O R I N
. . R A D . . P E N . .
F O R E V E R . C A T S P A W
E M I L A . A T U L . A R M A
T A L A N . H A L L . L E A K
A R E N A . L E L A . L Y R E
```

23

```
T O R S  [] S U M P S  [] C F O
A R I A  [] A G L A R E [] A R G
L T C M D R T U V O K  [] P O L
C H E K O V [] S A T [] E T N A
[] I N A D [] L E A P A T
U S E R S [] R E A C T O R []
L U N K [] T A X [] T O S C A T
A L S [] D R M C C O Y [] H U R
N U C L E I [] E A R [] C E R O
[] R A S C A L S [] A R R A Y
[] B U R T O N [] T I R E []
T U S K [] R I O [] N E W M A R
E M H [] A D M N A K A M U R A
A P E [] P E A C H Y [] A S T I
S S R [] A R L E S [] N E E D
```

24

```
S P A S [] M A S S E [] K T A L
H U R T [] A I L E D [] A H O Y
A M A R [] H R O M I [] T A K E
G A B A R O S T I S T E W []
[] S Y N O N [] S O I L []
[] G L E S S [] N E I M A N
Z A B E E N U T S [] S N O R E
I R E [] C A P [] R D A
N E A T H [] H L A K A S O U P
C A R H O P [] K R I G E []
[] E L A S [] N A V O T []
[] T R E L L A N C R E P E S
G O R O [] L I S E A [] N E L L
I D I C [] I D I N I [] T R O I
K O O K [] D E L E D [] H A S P
```

25

```
S A W N [] D I A N A [] W S W
O L E A [] C E N T E R [] O H O
U S S S A R A T O G A [] R I O
P O T A G E [] S L O [] E L A S
[] R U E R [] L T C M D R
R A F I N [] Y E S I A M []
E R A [] L A X [] A P E L L A
F A R P O I N T S T A T I O N
S T R O N G [] R A E [] E R N
[] S E H L A T [] B O N E S
[] A N S A T A [] O F I T []
B R A E [] S S A [] A L T A I R
E M H [] T H E B A D L A N D S
T I M [] S I R E N S [] W A L T
A N I [] U P S E T [] A P E S
```

26

```
B R A S H [] F O C A L [] H A J
R A S T A [] A L O N E [] A G A
O N I O N [] R E N D S [] Y E N
K A L I N T R O S E [] A N N E
[] C A W [] S C A R L E T T
E P I [] H E R [] I N A D []
B E L E [] R A V E [] Y A R K A
B R I N [] P O I N T [] R E O N
S T A T E [] V I C O [] A N N A
[] E L B A [] E T A [] E O N
S Y M B I O N T [] H R S []
E P E E [] S T E V E I H N A T
R O M [] E L I N E [] S A D I E
O R A [] D I K O N [] S L A D E
S A D [] S C A N T [] A L K A R
```

27

```
C A S K [] G A M E S [] Q O L
R E A L M [] A P O L O [] C R O
T O L I A N S O R A N [] O R S
[] N A N C Y [] S T Y [] D N A S
[] G A M S [] A S C O T []
A G L O W [] P E R I O D I C
W R E N [] C A N [] A D O N I S
N E A [] M A R T I N E [] U R E
S C H U S S [] R N S [] P U C E
[] O B S E S S E D [] E L M E R
[] R E C A P [] S O D A []
S T A R [] N R A [] A G N E S
H A H [] E D I T H K E E L E R
A R M [] A R N E B [] S T O N E
P G S [] R A G E R [] S I T O
```

28

```
C H E E [] P H I L [] S P I T E
H A L L [] L A N A [] A R N E B
A L A E [] O R R A [] K O R M A
D I S C O M M E N D A T I O N
[] T I E [] O R E []
S C A R L E T [] K R I S T A K
H E V A [] K A D A N [] T R U E
E L A [] R A P [] I R A
E L I M [] N O R E P [] A L A N
P O L E C A T [] C A M I L L E
[] A R F [] F O R []
S I N S O F T H E F A T H E R
A L O U D [] H A I R [] R E N E
I S E R E [] A N N A [] A R E S
D A L E N [] I D E N [] M O G H
```

29

```
S C A B . . T P E L . . J E T
T O L E . B R U M E . C E L L
A L I A . L E M A Y . O R S O
B U C K B O K A I . S L I E R
. M E S O N . . L I K O .
. . . I D I C . J A N I C E
B L I S S . T U R K . I L E S
R U M P E L S T I L T S K I N
A L A I . I O U S . A T A L E
T U N N E L . P A R K .
. . E T T E . . A E G I S
F A L L S . J A D Z I A D A X
I D O L . M E T O O . L I T E
E Z R I . A C T O R . E N O L
F E E . S T A R . . N I N O
```

30

```
P A P A S . M O R E . J E R I
U L A N I . A L E C . A D A R
F L U I D . R E E L . G O D S
F A L S E P R O F I T S .
. N I E C E . S P Y . N I A
. . A R T S . S E C O N D
E N T E R P R I S E . A R N E
R E E D . A M P . V E I L
I S L A . A P O C A L Y P S E
K T E M O C . N A M E .
A S K . D A L . A V E R Y
. I N D I S C R E T I O N
R I N N . E T T A . R A D U E
A T O A . M R E T . E N E R O
L O R D . Y E T O . D A R E N
```

31

```
L O G I C . L E A S . H A R A
I R I S H . A R T E . O R A L
D E L T A . K A T E . L O V E
S O L . K A T . A N I O N I C
. . O R I . C O R N .
I R E . T U V O K . K O M A R
B E N J A M I N . V I V A
A L L A Y . A A P . H E L E N
R E A D . R E D A L E R T
S E I Z E . M A N O R . S Y S
. . I N G A . T O R .
V O Y A G E R . A R Y . M E W
A P E D . S C A R . K O A L A
S E T A . S U L U . I D R A N
T R I X . O S E S . M O U S E
```

32

```
W A R P . D R O P . G O A T
I G O R . A A R E . T E R S A
N A M E . W M A R . A M S H A
K R A S . S A L T S H A K E R
. . S H O R . O J I .
T H E M A N T R A P . V A S H
R A B A L . A M U . M A E
O D A N . R E C A P . L A I C
V E N . O D E . J A R T H
E N D S . B O R G I A R O O T
. . A M I . A N B O .
B E A U R E G A R D . S E L F
A L I C E . E Z R I . I L I A
B I D E T . E N E G . A B E T
A M A R . S A T O . N A N E
```

33

```
S A T O . P A S T A . A T O R
E X E C . E L A A N . N A M U
V E R A . C A D R E . S K E W
E L I M G A R A K . E G O
. . P A N . T A L A X I A N
S T E A L . L I L Y .
D O G N A P . C I T I Z E N S
A R G . S A R A H . R E A
K E S P R Y T T . E F F E C T
. . T A C T . A L I K E
J O N A T H A N . T W O
U R E . C O R I N T H I V
M I R A . A K R E M . T A R E
J O Y S . M E S N E . E R O S
A N S A . T R E E S . R A N T
```

34

```
N A F F . S A R A . R A I F I
O R R A . P R A N . E R R E D
A D I N . A E O N . M T E L L
H U N T E R S . A R O E S T E
. . O R B . A R M .
C H A M B E R . W R A I T H S
L O R E . R O S I E . S H E A
A R A . M U L . R A N
I N Y O . K A L E B . M E R A
M E A S L E S . Y A R E E N A
. . M O R . J I L .
S A K O N N A . G O G A R T Y
E M O T E . L K O R . K A R O
C I V I L . M A R A . O N E S
T R A C Y . A R O N . N A S A
```

35

```
S U N U P   P A G H     T A S
A M A P A   I L I A   R E S H
S P U R N   C A N S   E L H I
    S I G M A   S H A T N E R
E M I S S A R Y   D I A N E
R I C E   I D A N I A N
I D A       N E D   A P I A
K R A G   L O K A I   L A D S
A O N E   A R E       R I C
    S K R R E E A   E T N A
A R O S E   S T A R S H I P
P E G A S U S   H A I K U
A G A R   S E T I   G I M M E
L E W D   A L E C   E M A I L
E R A     F A N S   L O N K A
```

36

```
S U L   C R O S I S   P L U M
E M I   H E G H T A   G I N A
R A M   E E L I E R   A B I T
F L I M F L A M M A N   E T E
S I T O       S H A R R
    B A T E S   G E T I N
L A D Y K I L L E R   V I C O
I R A   A N A Y D I S   N E D
S A N D   S L E I G H R I D E
A K A A R   R E S E E
    R E A L M       A N B O
I N A   L O C K A N D L O A D
S I P E   T H E T O E   O S E
A C E S   T A L I S A   N I L
K E L P   O R A T E D   E L L
```

37

```
R A F I N   T W O S   F A J O
E L I N E   R A M P   L I E S
F E R E N G I N A R   A D E S
    P E E N   N I A G A R A
  D S T   E N S I G N S
P O T   E E S   T H A R
I B E T   P E T   A S I M O V
A B R A   T R I K E   P A G E
F I E L D S   L I D   S N U G
  N O O R   L A R   D E A
    S U L I B A N   H A S
A N T I G E N   M E S O
M I L A   E N T E R P R I S E
A N O N   T E A R   O T N E R
S E R S   A T T U   T A N A S
```

38

```
R I O   C E T I   G E R A L D
E N D   A L A N   E K O R I A
C H O   I D I D   T O A T E E
R A I N R O B I N S O N
A L T O O N A   E R R A T I C
T E A M   K A V I   O R O
E D L O N G   R E D R O V E R
    R E A D Y R O O M
C A M E L L I A   F I E L D S
U S A   A N N A   K E E L
B A R C O D E   B A K L A V A
    R H O D E S R E A S O N
C A G I E R   R E E L   H U D
O G U S I I   O N N A   E R E
B E S T R I   S T A T   S S R
```

39

```
T W O S   G O L D   S A M E
P A R K   E R I E   P H L O X
A C T I   N A P S   E A T A T
N O O N I E N S O O N G
    O E R   T U T   C O M
  Z E F R A M C O C H R A N E
B I N   L O O   H O U S E S
U P D O S   M M V   R E T C H
S P I R E A   I C H   L A Y
B E V E R L Y C R U S H E R
Y D E   P T O   N A E
    L E O N A R D M C C O Y
B R A I N   A J A R   T A V A
R O G E T   D A T E   O M A R
A M E N   A X E D   R E L S
```

40

```
C H R I S   M A G I   H I D E
L E A N S   I D I C   E L A N
A L I C E K R I G E   A O N E
R E F   S O O N   W A R N O G
K R I S T A K   H A R T
    C A N   M A T T O C K
M O L O R   P I N E   F A N S
A L O T   A L T A R   T R E E
G A L T   G A R R   H A Y E K
  F A B R I N A   M E R
    A U T O   M O R G A N A
O M E K L A   L A N A   S A R
M A R U   T R A N S L A T O R
A X I L   O A H U   D R E M A
G I N A   R U R A   S A R I S
```

41

```
A L E C _ _ O D A L A _ Y A R
L I D O _ D R A M A S _ A G A
P L O M E E K S O U P _ M I N
S I M P L E _ H E R _ R O L K
_ _ T A P S _ B E L I K E _ _
_ N C O S _ I T A L I C S _ _
J O H N _ M G R _ I D E A T E
A V E _ L I N A L A S _ U P A
R A C H E L _ I O N _ S C A R
_ H A I L I N G _ C H E N _ _
_ S T A S I S _ S U L U _ _ _
A L L S _ P R E _ S E T T O S
L I U _ H E A R T O F T A R G
A P T _ A D E L E S _ L I A T
I S H _ H E L E N _ E L L S _
```

42

```
I L O S E _ D K E L _ T A S S
V I R A L _ R O P E _ A T U L
A T R I A _ O P E N _ M A L A
R E A L M O F F E A R _ R A D
_ _ _ O D O _ _ K E A N E _ _
A P P O S E _ S E R A N _ _ _
B E A U _ G U L H A D A R _ _
C A P T A I N S H O L I D A Y
_ Y A D E R A I I _ N A V E _
_ _ I R A T E _ R E G R E T _
B A N D I _ _ D A R _ _ _ _ _
A L A _ E N E M Y W I T H I N
B Y R D _ A V E L _ D I A N E
E C R U _ M I R A _ O R I A S
L E A D _ E L A N _ N E R D S
```

43

```
F R I L L _ J E T _ P R A K
L E N T O _ O T E L _ R O S A
Y E A R O F H E L L _ O A S T
E S L _ F A N _ L A M P R E Y
R E L O A D _ D U M A H _ _ _
_ _ T H E M E N A G E R I E
A D I T _ I M F _ M T E L L
C A T _ I N D I A N A _ N I A
A T E I N _ A N O _ T E A S
D A R K F R O N T I E R _ _
_ _ A R E N T _ S M I L E S
C O N T A C T _ P E P _ O C A
T R O I _ T I M E S A R R O W
R E E K _ O M A G _ T O I L E
S O L A _ E N S _ H O N E D
```

44

```
F R E Y A _ R O V E D _ B R Y
L E N I N _ O N A R A _ L O A
A M O N G _ B I G G S _ I A N
M I S T E R E A R S _ A N N A
_ _ _ L U R S A _ A L K A R
_ C O B A L T _ D N A _ _ _
R A R E _ S U S A N _ Z I O
D A G G E R O F T H E M I N D
A N Y _ L E N O R _ E T A N
_ _ A L E _ U N P A I D _ _
B O H N E _ S A Y R E _ _ _
A R I D _ V U L C A N H A R P
S I C _ R A Z I K _ T O V O R
T A K _ E L I N E _ H R O M I
E S S _ S T E E N _ E N N A N
```

45

```
L A C T O _ T P E L _ R M O R
E Q U A L _ O I L S _ I A N A
V U L C A N D E A T H G R I P
Y A S H _ D O R N _ A E T N A
_ _ _ Y E A _ _ I L L _ _ _
_ C L O A K I N G D E V I C E
B R U N T _ D E A L _ D I D
E A R _ S H I R L E Y _ A G E
E S S _ E N Y O _ I S H A N
P H A S E D I S R U P T O R
_ _ C R Y _ _ P E A _ _ _
S U T O K _ A T T U _ R I S A
P H O T O N T O R P E D O E S
A U N T _ C O N E _ D O N A T
T H E Y _ O M S K _ U M A N I
```

46

```
W R A T H _ M A I N _ B I K O
H O B I I _ A R C O _ O T A R
E M E N D _ U N I T _ R O G A
W A L T E R K O E N I G _ _ _
_ _ _ S K I _ R E D D E S T
M A C _ I C E T _ W A R N E R
A M A L _ O L E O _ H O R N E
R E N E A U B E R J O N O I S
T R U E S _ E T N A _ E L L S
H O T D O G _ H E R B _ S E A
A N T E N N A _ _ E E L _ _ _
_ _ L E O N A R D N I M O Y
J A N A _ M A R U _ Z A I R E
E T A N _ O R E S _ A N N E L
V E T O _ N A S H _ R A D O N
```

47

```
BAGS    MAST     TKL
ELREM   OLEIC    RAE
YOUCANTFREE      ITE
SUB   REHAB   LASER
     ASWE   KIRK
AFISHFROMWATER
ERNIE    DEA    LIN
OAT   SAKONNA   INO
NNE   NAR    BOONE
 GREEDISETERNAL
  PENA   LETS
ACHED   SLANT   EDS
MOA   EXPANDORDIE
ADS   DARIN   RIGEL
REE    TYRA    BETA
```

48

```
ERIC   RANA   STALK
YURO   ARAL   HALEE
ELIM   HERB   ANDGO
DESPERATION   EEG
    EVA   HEATRASH
HONTIHL    THE
AREEL   ISAHIGHLY
LUM   PEERS   AES
EMOTIONAL   GAUGE
   ARI   OCONNOR
FLAMENCO   LOO
LOG   STATEOFMIND
ATROI   IRAN   ANGE
STERN   RISE   LYON
KEENE   ONES   YOST
```

49

```
WISH   ODIN   SPRAT
ASHE   ROSA   PLANA
REON   GOSS   LONAR
PROGRAM   ADAMANT
   IAN   OSE
PRISHIC   BOHEEKA
HURT   AHDAR   KLEG
ASE   END   ANA
SONA   FLAGS   ANDI
ETERNAL   ETANIAN
   AAR   ARC
CHANCES   EPSILON
HELDE   YELL   EINE
ARLIN   BABE   NANA
NOISE   OTAR   TRAP
```

50

```
TAS   AMONG   SCAR
ATP   LEVAR   HERNE
SHOCKWAVE   EMONY
MOCHAS   AFRICA
   SKIN   OSTEO
   LEECH   WITHIN
RIND   ETAS   SHORE
STARTREKNEMESIS
VANER   TAAR   REST
PLANET   AKIRA
   LORRE   EVIL
HIKARU   EVENED
CORIN   BROKENBOW
AWARE   LENOR   ELI
PENK   ELISE   DAS
```